GOTHIC OLYMPUS

“That which never happened is eternally true.”

— Emperor Julian the Apostate

Gothic Olympus

CHRISTIAN CHENSVOLD

ARKTOS
LONDON 2026

ARKTOS

Arktos.com fb.com/Arktos arktosmedia arktosjournal

The Author extends his gratitude to Nick Willard.

ISBN

978-1-918418-14-9 (Paperback)
978-1-918418-15-6 (Hardback)
978-1-918418-16-3 (Ebook)

Editing

Jafe Arnold

Layout and Cover

Tor Westman

To the Germanic astrologers
on my Mother's side:
Carolyn Sue, Edna Marie, Ida May
& Leonard

OVERTURE

In reading this book you consent to play The Game. It's called Decadence, and there's a catch.

It has already begun, you see, and you must play whether you like it or not.

The Supreme Author has decreed a time and purpose for everything. The fairest damsel, placed inside a rosewood casket and laid to rest in a marble mausoleum, will still be devoured by worms. And her valiant beau, that swashbuckling swain with a wrist of steel, will one day lose his last duel to the Grim Reaper, who will arrive at the foggy field by dawn's early light to claim his pre-ordained victory.

Every carefree summer must succumb to autumnal lament, and leaves fall from the trees just to be ground into dust beneath the snows of winter.

If only we could stop the process, fix the final sunset of the ripest day, would that not be immortality? What if a civilization at the edge of the abyss were not to collapse, but rather ensconced itself in an everlasting glass-shielded globe-world of beauty?

Even if dark magic were required to defy cosmic law, would it not in fact honor The Creator by saving the world from folly, stupidity, and ubiquitous ugliness? Then a *Belle Époque* could reign forever.

In times of upheaval it is difficult to understand what is happening, even as it unfolds before one's eyes. Once again nature provides the analogy, for spring buds do not burst forth while they are being watched, nor do winter trees become barren all at once. Mankind goes about its business oblivious to the changes happening beneath the level of observation, and only notices the cherry blossoms when they are in full bloom.

And so when one hears of a goblin scurrying down a dark alley or someone is suspected of being in league with the Devil, no one pays attention to such rumors, for people have always thought such things.

But after finally accepting that they are trapped inside The Game That Must Be Played, the people of Europa will want to pour a glass of absinthe to drown their sorrows.

But they will not be able to, and will beg the green fairy to take them somewhere far away.

CHAPTER ONE

ROBERTSON DESCENDED the staircase leading to the bowels of Wishing Well, where New York night-crawlers came to slake their thirst for flesh and appetite for oblivion. Parting a set of crimson curtains, he entered a parlor filled with men in evening clothes and women in stockings and corsets, walking timidly across a sticky floor that clung to his every step like a gaudy gremlin from some unctuous underworld.

Being a man of devout faith, Robertson resented this late-night errand to the Bowery's most notorious den of iniquity. But Madame Stanwyck was the most generous tenant at the Gramercy Park building where he worked, and he had grown fond of the celebrated stage actress. But her dissolute son was another matter. Madame had spared no expense in his education, but from what Robertson could tell all the young man ever did was loaf by day and carouse by night as though a member of the nobility.

Robertson spied Julien Stanwyck across the smoke-filled room, his shirt audaciously undone to reveal the ghostly pallor of his skin. He took a seat at a tarnished piano, placing upon its weatherbeaten wood a half-empty bottle of cognac. With a gesture Robertson found revolting, Julien ran his ring-covered fingers through his long chestnut hair, and proceeded to draw from the ill-tuned instrument agitated tones harmonized on the Devil's Interval.

Three disreputable ladies surrounded Julien, and Robertson—as though the gremlin of the floor had succeeded in rendering him immobile—found himself watching spellbound as Madame Stanwyck's son sang to the feminine trio, coaxing sweet sighs from them for accompaniment:

Your face is a cryptic poem written in runes
An indigo graveyard for two melancholy moons
The songs of your soul shine forth with their beams
And are understood only by cats in their dreams

The ocean recoils from the depth of your stare
Afraid of the mysteries that lie brooding there
And the sky is jealous of all you conceal
Behind those blue eyes that mask all you feel

Porcelain lily, your gaze exudes incense
Your eyes like clouds of smoke moist and dense
What do you hide behind those blue marble balls?
That you feel like a flower on which rain never falls?

"You move me to tears," gushed one of Julien's admirers.

"Is it about me?" wondered the second.

"If it was about me," said the third, stroking him like a homeless cat, "it wouldn't be about my eyes."

Robertson shook off his enchantment and pushed through the crowd. "Mr. Stanwyck," he said, "it's your mother. I'm afraid she's taken a turn for the worse. The priest has been called."

Julien's response was so stoic Robertson wondered if he had not been heard above the raucous din, and repeated himself.

"I heard you the first time!" Julien shouted, rising from the piano and knocking over the bench. He seized the cognac, poured the amber liquid down his throat, then hurled the bottle into a mirror while emitting a primal scream from the same voice that moments before had given such a tender serenade.

Everyone in the building was aware of Julien's return, so heavy were his boot-steps as he stormed through the door and bounded up the stairs. Anne Stanwyck was famous for her melodramatic death scenes, which she had played to packed houses in every corner of the civilized world. But now that life required her to enact her own ending, her words became terse and her gestures sparse.

She embraced her kneeling son's face, sliding her frail hand from his wet cheeks to his flowing locks, and looked deep into his burning eyes. "Listen, my love. There is a way for you to never worry about money again. It pertains to your father."

"You were never good with numbers, mother," said Julien. "Considering I was born on the twelfth of April, 1872, I doubt my father was killed in the Civil War."

"And you were so sweet for playing along with me all these years," Madame Stanwyck said through a viscous cough, "but now you must know the truth. I met your real father in Paris; that is why your name is spelled with an E, and why I made you study French. You are a love child, my darling, though love played no role in your conception, for I was taken against my will. But from that violation a beautiful boy was born, with a face for the Old Masters and a voice for a heavenly choir."

Madame Stanwyck struggled to lift herself higher against the pillows supporting her. "There is more, Julien. When your father died, I asked our lawyer to investigate. In the Kingdom of Gaul, according to the rights of primogeniture, even a bastard may inherit a noble estate. My dear boy, you are the Comte de la Tour-Abolie."

"Count of the Ruined Tower…" muttered Julien.

"Have you nothing to say?"

"I don't understand. What is it you wish me to do?"

"Take what is yours," replied Madame Stanwyck. "Redeem the evil committed against your mother."

As her voice grew weaker, Madame Stanwyck explained that an envelope on her dresser contained all the necessary documentation for Julien to lay claim to the estate of Tour-Abolie. There was also a contact waiting for him, as Madame's dearest friend of the French stage had a son the same age as Julien who had studied law.

A quarter of an hour later she closed her eyes and gasped her last breath.

After the funeral Julien walked aimlessly through the blustery morning until he found himself in The Battery. He sat on a frigid bench and let his eyes wander over the Upper Bay until they landed on Lady Liberty, that great gift of Gaul bequeathed in 1876. He had looked at her often, but, if she looked different today, it was because different eyes were gazing at her.

In a mysterious sliver of silence wedged between moments, Julien felt he could hear Lady Liberty speak. "Go to the Old World," she seemed to say with her torch pointed towards the sky. "As your mother told you."

Julien reluctantly accepted that there was something he must do, even if he didn't know how he would accomplish it. There was certainly no one to help him: he was completely friendless, having judged the elegant vapid, the learned pedestrian, and the artistic undignified. As for women, his love affairs had been a cross between wanton philandering and vampiric extractions of their feminine essence.

As far as anything resembling a vocation went, Madame Stanwyck had been complicit in her son's wish to be a man of leisure, so contemptuous was he of entanglements with the marketplace. But she had spoken the truth when she said that Julien's voice was angelic. Deep in the night, in the dark dives he frequented, the response to his music often disturbed him. How fitting, Julien thought to himself, that he should have been brought into the world through an act of violation, given how often he cursed fate that he had ever been born.

And then, for the thousandth time, Julien wondered why he had come so late upon the world stage. Would his soul have been less troubled had he been born in a more heroic age? Rising from his reveries, he began the long walk home, his boots echoing on the pavement until their sound was overcome by a newspaper boy hawking the afternoon edition.

"Read all about it!" he shouted. "Gargoyles ransack Paris!"

So fantastic were the boy's words that Julien handed him a coin.

According to the paper, several women claimed to have seen gargoyles tear themselves from the cathedral of Notre Dame, smash the stained-glass windows, and fly off into the night. Authorities attributed the vandalism to the recent spate of anarchist activities, and chalked up the flying monsters to the runaway imagination of the witnesses, who were pious old ladies fresh from evening vespers.

Julien shook his head and promptly disposed of the wretched tabloid.

It did not take long for him to liquidate the contents of the Gramercy Park apartment he'd shared with his mother. Although the uncertain future troubled him, something inside said he may never return. He packed three steamer trunks, cracking a droll grin at the thought of labeling them body, soul and spirit. The first held his clothing, boots and toiletries, while the second carried his books, writings, and mementos.

The third trunk, corresponding to spirit, was empty, to be filled at a later date with contents as yet unknown.

CHAPTER TWO

JULIEN'S SECOND-CLASS ticket on the *SS Saint George* provided suitable accommodations, but it was still a cell within a floating prison in the middle of the ocean. It would take 12 days to reach the sceptered isle of Albion, and his state of mind for the first seven such intervals followed a pattern familiar to initiates of the Mysteries.

Julien spent the first day in fear, as each roll of the ship brought out a reaction in him akin to that of a skittish cat. Just a gentle jostle and his imagination would conjure up maelstroms straight from the pen of Edgar Poe, with agonizing nausea and passengers run amok like lunatics. No amount of rum brought rest that night, and as he strolled the deck on the morning of the second day he slipped into a state of spleen. Banging his head, he cursed every feature of the ship's design, and found the food inedible even though he had no appetite.

On the third day Julien felt like a child and spent the day weeping for his sad lot in life. But on day four he developed his sea legs, and word from the captain was that the voyage would be smooth. Julien spent the day in a state of boredom, slept for twelve hours, and awoke on the fifth day with his eyes wide and manic.

His mother was dead, he had no home, and he was trapped in the middle of the Atlantic. Whether he curled into a ball or stood at the prow in hopes that a bitter breeze would calm him, nothing could stave off the feeling of looming madness. He sweated all through the night and rose on the sixth day in the shadow of death.

Julien couldn't take it anymore. The voyage was interminable, the agony unbearable. He spent the entire day and night debating the most efficient way to end his life, but his arguments and counter-arguments never found a resolution, and just before dawn he finally fell asleep from sheer exhaustion.

On the seventh day Julien awoke feeling like a child who had gotten through a long illness and could finally go outside and play. He was traveling on an ocean liner and there was simply nothing he could do about it. Besides, he was now more than halfway there, and the thought of it actually excited him. His maiden sea voyage! The Old World! The Count of the Ruined Tower!

He spent the next few days in a state of mounting vigor, eventually finding himself in the recreation room. For as fond as he was of drink, Julien kept a strict exercise regimen in order to maintain his 28-inch waist. And since nothing was more becoming on a tall young man with long hair and a chiseled face than a pair of broad shoulders, Julien grabbed a pair of barbells and set about maintaining a layer of muscle on his svelte skeleton.

Grimacing from the exertion, and with beads of sweat dripping down his unshaven face, Julien's eyes settled on the silliest thing he had ever seen. Across the room a mahogany dining table was split in half by a six-inch net. Drowning in gray athletic garb, an effeminate kid was smacking a white ball with a paddle that looked like it was used for administering corporal punishment to recalcitrant toddlers.

When his last opponent had left the room in defeat, the kid waved Julien over with a mischievous smile, saying the game was really quite fun.

"Fun?" Julien replied, drying himself with a terrycloth towel. "What's that?"

"Come on," said the lad, "what else are you going to do in this floating prison?"

The description of the *SS Saint George* made Julien chuckle, and so he decided to humor the kid. The ball came bounding to his side of the table, and Julien met it with a gust of wind.

"That's called a swing and a miss," the kid laughed.

When the next serve bounced towards him, Julien once again swun with all his might, this time catching the ball on the edge of the paddle, causing it to ricochet into his nose.

"That one there's no name for!"

Julien threw down the paddle and promptly left. After napping through the afternoon, he awoke with a hearty appetite—and for more than just food.

The first thing to do was remove his pirate stubble. When his face was as pale and glabrous as a full moon, Julien splashed on some amber-scented *eau de parfum*, put on his coat *sans cravat*, and ate a leisurely meal in the ship's dining hall. Afterwards he sipped cognac in the lounge while humming lugubrious melodies, waiting like a spider for a fetching damsel to arrive.

As midnight approached only a few souls remained in the wood-paneled room. It was then Julien fixed upon an unusual young girl who had been watching him surreptitiously, her eyes darting up to peek at him before returning to what looked to be a sketchbook. When she peered up and found Julien staring back at her, the girl smiled shyly.

She was a kind of pixie —a *gamine,* if Julien recalled the expression correctly—with the face of a lovely maid but hair cropped like a boy's.

"You clean up well," the girl said from across the room. "But doesn't it hurt?"

"Not if you keep the razor sharp," Julien replied, taking cavalier strides to join her.

"I mean, if your face hurts that much to look at," she said, "I can't imagine what it's like to be its owner. You're some kind of freak. Even girls aren't that pretty."

Julien smiled awkwardly with the self-deprecation that came whenever anyone remarked on his looks.

Introducing herself as Zoe Wingate from the Hudson Valley, the girl wore skin-tight trousers like a gentleman from the Regency, which were tucked into black boots of feminine shape with a pointed toe and scalloped heel. Her black coat was styled like a man's but sculpted to her subtle curves, and her torso was clad in an ivory tight lace top with a tall collar. A strand of pearls fell in a V-line between her taut breasts, which were uninhibited by any other layer of fabric between lace top and rosy skin. She admitted that she had been drawing Julien, who asked to see the image.

It showed a regal figure that looked like Julien's distant relative, framed by a Gothic window and Grecian key motif. The rest of the page was covered with strange symbols suggesting arcane knowledge, causing Julien to facetiously inquire whether she were some kind of witch.

"Swing and a miss!" replied the girl.

Julien stared at her. "I don't believe it," he deadpanned. "That's impossible. And that room is for gentlemen, you know."

"Then what were *you* doing there?"

Julien laughed out loud, and Zoe went on to explain that the parlor game was all the rage at Barnard, which she had left in order to embark unchaperoned on a "secret mission" to the Old World. When the barkeep said he was closing the lounge, Julien offered to escort the young lady to her cabin.

"I'm afraid you'd frighten any dowagers who might see you, Mr. Stanwyck," she said. "You see, I have a first-class ticket."

"Tomorrow night, then?"

"Yes, the magic number is 22."

"Is that how old you are? But you don't look a day over 18."

"I am indeed 22, and it's also the hour at which you'll find me here. Then, perhaps, I'll tell you the third reason why it's the magic number."

"Let me guess," Julien teased. "You're an heiress worth $22 million off to buy a noble title? A European count may be closer than you think."

Julien woke late the following day after a restless night. The quirky girl-boy had lodged herself in Julien's imagination, which was conjuring all sorts of deliciously wicked things he would do to her once she surrendered, which had to be that night, for the following day they would reach Southampton. There was one way to ensure victory, and so Julien prowled the ship in search of a piano. There was one in the first-class dining hall, a steward informed him, which closed at 10. Julien's seductive siege would thus consist of drinks in the lounge and a walk in the moonlight, followed by the sheer happenstance of stumbling upon the vacant dining hall. By the third song Zoe would be all but dragging him to her cabin to be deflowered.

At 10 past 10 Julien entered the lounge where he found Zoe in a state of agitation over her sketchbook, as if she were not present to herself and were drawing automatically. Julien asked what ailed her, and she handed him the sketchbook, where page after page showed the same thing: a lightning bolt shooting down from the sky and splitting a ship in two.

"It started this afternoon," said Zoe, as if describing a sudden illness. "I haven't been able to stop."

Julien examined the images more closely. Sometimes the lightning was shown hovering over the vessel, sometimes striking it, and sometimes it was reduced to floating debris. But in each instance — whether woven into lightning bolts, emblazoned on the ship, or in the whirlpool of its sinking — was the same number: 16.

"What does this mean?" he asked.

"Remember yesterday when I told you about the magic number 22, that it's my age, the hour for us to meet tonight, and another thing? The third thing is that 22 is the number of cards in the Book of Tarot. The sixteenth card is called The Tower. It means misfortune, catastrophe, and is usually depicted as a lightning bolt striking a castle. Have you heard of Zapfe?"

Julien shook his head.

"Zapfe is who I'm going to meet in the Old World," Zoe explained. "He has a castle high in the Alps. I sent him some of my drawings, and he wants to collaborate on a new set of cards."

"Let me get this straight," said Julien. "You're going unchaperoned to a remote mountain castle to meet a wizard whose name starts with a Z?"

"But my name starts with Z," said Zoe. "Besides, I won't be alone. He's the leader of a secret spiritual order."

Julien let out an agitated sigh. "They'll have to fatten you up before roasting you over the fire, Miss Wingate."

"Why is everything misanthropy with you?" said Zoe, before tottering as if dizzy.

The rolling of the ship was clearly not the cause of her disorientation, and Julien ordered her to go lie down. Zoe held her sketchbook in one arm and entwined the other with Julien's as the pair weaved through the ship's labyrinthine interior towards first class.

When they reached a T intersection Zoe said her room was to the right, but Julien spied a plaque indicating the Dining Hall. He turned left, saying there was something that would cheer her up. Zoe said she wasn't hungry and that it was closed anyway, but her pixie demeanor returned when Julien seated her in front of the stage and climbed up to the piano which stood upon its darkened floorboards.

He sounded a series of lugubrious chords which transitioned into a fireworks display of arpeggios before quieting to *pianissimo*, at which point he opened his mouth and unsheathed the voice of a fallen angel:

The withered leaves of autumn
In silence dare to fly
On waves of a capricious wind
Which leads them but to die

No more mere ornaments,
With final arboreal breath
They seek to imitate the birds
And plummet to their death

I'll too surrender to that wind
When you and I are parted
And I must cease to know you
Before I've even started

Julien's final chord lent the piece a feeling of uncertainty. He brushed away the flowing locks that fell from his bowed head, and looked up, jaw askew with primordial hunger.

A burst of light shone across the dark hall from an open door in which Zoe stood, silhouetted against the light of the hallway and looking back at Julien. She disappeared into the ship's labyrinth, and Julien followed in hot pursuit. In the hallway she slid past a plump bourgeois and his wife, then out the door to lean against the railing, facing the roaring sea.

Julien crept slowly towards her, asking why she had left without a word. Zoe's head dropped and shook from side to side. The angle of her neck inflamed Julien, and his eyes worked downward to take in the arch of her back and shape of her hips. He put his hands on the railing on either side of her, and Zoe felt them as both pillars of strength and bars of bondage meant to extract a confession.

"It's our last night together," said Julien, his breath landing on her ear. "Why don't you turn around and face me?"

"Because I know you'll kiss me," Zoe sighed. Slowly she turned with her head still bowed, but when Julien began to lift her chin with his finger, she dug her nails into his flanks, tickled wildly, and escaped.

"Tomorrow, there's something we must do," she said.

"I know," Julien replied suggestively.

"I'll send for you when I'm ready," Zoe flushed. "Good night, sweet prince!" And she giggled off into the night.

The following day a porter delivered Julien a note requesting his presence in the tea room at 4. The *Saint George* was scheduled to make port soon after, so Julien resigned himself to the notion that a dalliance at sea was impossible. If the strange feelings Zoe had aroused in him called for a consummation, he realized he would need to move on to a long-term strategy.

Julien arrived in the tea room to find Zoe a model of respectability for their arrival in Albion. He slumped into his chair and promptly celebrated the end of the interminable voyage.

"Come now," said Zoe, "was it really so bad?"

"Your company was the sole consolation, Miss Wingate."

"Seconded," Zoe said with a mock-gracious nod. She then removed a deck of cards and fanned them on the table. "I think I should give you a Tarot reading. I feel the cards will help you navigate the adventure that awaits."

Julien indicated his lack of interest with a foppish toss of his hair.

"Tarot's origins are unknown," explained Zoe, ignoring him, "but its power to stimulate the imagination suggests a direct link with the higher intelligence that structures reality. As a poet, I think you'll be intrigued.

"Now there are 22 cards in what's called the Major Arcana," she continued. "This deck was designed a few years ago by a man named Oswald Wirth. We'll do a seven-card spread representing your adventure in the Old World. If you're ever confused just remember the cards, for fate will lead your selection, and they will guide your subconscious mind."

Zoe gestured to the cards. Julien selected seven of them, asking if he should look at them. Zoe suggested that he turn them over one at a time, and so Julien commenced the reading by turning over the card called Death. His affected ennui turned bitter, and he said he no longer wished to play.

"It doesn't mean you or anyone else is going to die," Zoe stressed. "It just means the end of something."

Julien proceeded to turn over The Priestess, followed by card 16, The Tower. Zoe gasped, regained her composure, and told him to continue. Julien went on to reveal The Hermit, The Lovers, The Devil and The Emperor. Zoe suggested Julien write them down, but he said he'd memorize them before asking what they meant.

"I think it's the story of a transformative journey. It begins with the end of something, and ends with a beginning. In this case, of a new kingdom, a new life. Anyway, I'm sure you're in for an incredible adventure. Someone like you must have a great destiny in store, otherwise you wouldn't be as you are."

Then Zoe told him to select one more card for his eyes only, which would help guide his interpretation of the others when the time was right. Julien did as she requested just as a passenger entered the tea room shouting "Land ho!"

Julien suggested they join the madding crowd and take their first look at the Sceptered Isle, but Zoe asked about the song he sung the night before, and why he had chosen it.

"I could barely see and the chords are simple."

"That's it? What about the last line? About ceasing to know me before we've even started. Are we never to see each other again?"

"You have a mission," said Julien stoically. "A Zapfe. In fact, that's what I think I'll call it. You have a Zapfe to fulfill."

They stepped into the late afternoon, jostling with the crowd while exchanging itineraries. Zoe intended to sail to Cherbourg, while Julien had settled on the train to Londontown, followed by the ferry to Calais. With a warm smile she agreed to join him on his route, and the pair climbed up a staircase to a less-crowded perch on the upper deck, leaned against the railing, and took in their first sight of land in 12 days.

"I feel silly about last night," confessed Zoe. "Running off like that. But the music, the poetry, your voice… Doors will open for you, Julien. And not just salon doors. Palace doors."

"I'm not interested in anything like that," Julien said haughtily. "I have my own 'Zapfe' to fulfill."

"Well I don't know about you, but I'm dying for a hot bath and a warm meal," Zoe said, stretching her arms and freezing mid-stretch at the sound of a loud clamor.

The pair searched for the source of the disturbance and soon found it. On the deck directly below a man stood perched on the railing, shouting words of villainy and spite. After waving his arms in some kind of infernal invocation, he pressed a pistol to the side of his head and sent a shower of grey matter onto the passengers below.

Their screams were immediately drowned out by a thunderous boom from the ship's prow, which caused the *Saint George* to violently roll. A moment later there came another blast, followed by a third and a fourth, all at regularly spaced intervals along the entire length of the ship. The fifth was near enough for Julien and Zoe to see timber and bodies flying in a volcanic explosion of destruction.

There was nothing to ponder, no options to weigh. Julien and Zoe's eyes met, and each saw mirrored in the other an absolute terror combined with the will to live. In a heartbeat they were standing on the other side of the railing, and a beat later they released their hold on the *Saint George*.

During their free-fall, Julien and Zoe experienced a moment of eternity. Neither alive nor dead, they had no thoughts, memories, or identity. They were simply beings who, unbeknownst to themselves, had been chosen for a higher purpose. When they splashed into the freezing waters the sacrifice was complete, and when they rose to the surface, their bursting lungs took the first breath of their new lives as children favored by the gods.

CHAPTER THREE

"THIS IS DISGUSTING," Julien growled as he opened the door.

"What is?" Zoe asked as she entered.

"Gin."

"Then stop drinking it," she said, grabbing the glass, "and quit stalling."

Julien nodded like a child forced to visit the dentist. He was wearing a clean white shirt graciously offered by the Hotel Southampton, but was wearing his own coat and trousers, which the sea had shrunk to the point they hugged his haggard physique like a second skin. At his request the concierge had managed to find a beaver top hat and sun-shading eyeglasses. With mock courtesy Julien offered his arm, which Zoe accepted with a genteel nod. The pair descended the staircase and entered the lobby, where they were met by several constables and the portly hotel manager, a certain Mr. Edgeworth, who led them to a crowded state room.

It had been three days of questioning from the maritime authorities, and now the sole survivors of the *SS Saint George* disaster had to face a firing squad of reporters who had already dubbed them "the Handsome Devil" and "the Tarot Tomboy." Edgeworth had previously worked as an auctioneer for bankrupt dandies, and sought to maintain order as the reporters' queries ricocheted across the room.

"Which is which?"

"Come on, Stanwyck, show us your pretty face!"

"Are the two of you engaged?"

"He hasn't asked yet," replied Zoe, tactfully responding to their inquiries while Julien sat motionless beneath his hat and sun-shades.

After half an hour of tedious questions fielded by Zoe, Edgeworth announced the conference would be ending, but a gentleman of the press said he had heard Julien was something of a musician.

"The description is accurate," Julien replied drily.

"Will you be entertaining us?"

"That will be announced at a later date," said an anonymous man from the crowd.

Julien and Zoe exchanged glances as they were whisked away into a nearby lounge for tea and refreshments. Zoe thanked Edgeworth for the accommodations; he replied that it was an honor to host the two Americans who were the talk of the kingdom, and whose presence had provided a reprieve from the tragedy of the many souls lost at sea — as well as a pleasant uptick in business.

Edgeworth went on to introduce Simon Asquith — the man who interjected himself at the close of the press conference — who reached into the chest pocket of his dove-gray suit, ruffling his yellow cravat, and produced a calling card. In a typeface of shameless flamboyance, it identified his profession as theatrical agent.

"I booked Oscar Wilde's lecture tour in the New World back in '82," Asquith boasted. "Perhaps you saw him? Anyway, I'd love to sell an exclusive to one of our high-circulation periodicals, the harrowing tale of the sole survivors saved by God."

"But all we did was hold wreckage until the rescue boats arrived," said Zoe.

"Figurines then?"

"Figurines?" queried Julien.

"Your likeness on dolls," explained Asquith. "Floating dolls for the tub, sold at fine apothecaries alongside soaps and bath salts. Really, Mr. Stanwyck, you'll have to pardon me, but your appearance. It's as if you'd leapt from the pages of Lord Byron to haunt the fantasies of young maidens, who'd love the chance to bathe with you."

"We've had a very trying time, Mr. Asquith," Zoe said diplomatically, "and are eager to resume our travels."

Asquith asked where, and when Zoe explained that they had hoped to catch a train to Londontown that evening, Asquith offered accommodations at his gentleman's club named Poodle's, and they could "brainstorm marketing possibilities" while riding up together.

Before Julien could say anything, Zoe took him aside. Given how eager they both were to reach the continent and leave the tragic voyage behind them, she reasoned, accepting the charity of a local might very well expedite their journey. The man could also help with other mundane matters, for while Julien had preserved his billfold in his coat pocket, Zoe would need to transfer funds at a bank.

Julien nodded and Zoe announced that they would be happy to accept Asquith's kindness. The showman booked three first-class tickets on the evening train and returned with a coach. The carriage ride raised Zoe's spirits, as the trotting horse-hooves made her feel as though the ordeal of the *Saint George* was finally over and she could begin to process what had happened—chiefly, the vision she had drawn obsessively in her notebook, only to see it come to pass.

Just as the train was about to leave the station, Asquith spied something on the platform and leapt from his seat. Julien and Zoe watched in befuddlement as he disappeared, becoming visible again on the platform as the train began moving, then returned to their compartment frantically out of breath. Smiling, he held in his hands the evening edition of the newspaper, but his smile vanished the moment he opened it. When he denounced it as rubbish and folded it, Zoe snatched it from him.

On the front page was a caricature of her and Julien beneath the headline "Demons in Disguise?" Zoe showed it to Julien, who laughed sardonically.

"They certainly don't believe we had nothing to do with it," she muttered while skimming the story.

"That's because the investigation has been inconclusive," said Asquith. "Edgeworth confided that at least one investigator believes it was an inside job."

"Why would they blow up their own ship and murder all those people?" wondered Zoe.

"Greed," Julien deadpanned.

"It's true people will do anything for money," said Asquith, drawing a sharp look from Julien. Pivoting, he suggested they go to the dining car, and Zoe said they would join him presently.

"You'd better hope your notebook doesn't wash up on shore," said Julien cynically.

Zoe fell silent, brow furrowed, and said she wanted Julien to give her a Tarot reading. He called the cards a terrible curse and told her that they belonged at the bottom of the sea. But Zoe produced her crinkled deck, which she credited to wearing gentlemen's trousers. She had Julien fan out the cards, explaining that they would do a four-card spread to help her understand the act of predestination she had drawn. The cards would stand for situation, obstacle, action and resolution.

Zoe closed her eyes and floated her hand over the cards before pointing her index finger downward. "This one," she said without opening her eyes. "Turn it face up."

Julien did as he was told, revealing card 16, The Tower.

Zoe opened her eyes and turned pale.

"I told you this was a bad idea," Julien protested.

Zoe forced him to continue, revealing The Lovers as her obstacle card, The Priestess as action to be taken, and, for the resolution, The Stars.

"Thank you," she said perfunctorily, gathering the deck. "Shall we join Mr. Asquith?"

The pair made their way to the dining car. Irked by the stares and whispers of his fellow passengers, Julien, still in top hat and sun-shades, stared quietly out the window while Zoe and Asquith engaged in small talk.

When the crowd finally thinned out, relieving Julien's agitation, he sighed and turned to his companions. They smiled politely at his presence, as though he had returned from another dimension, and Asquith said he understood that Julien was a musician by profession.

"I have no profession," Julien replied. "The authorities asked me what I do, and that's what I told them."

Asquith said he would certainly find an appreciative audience at Poodle's, causing Zoe to inquire about the club's history. The showman said it was a relatively new club—founded in the 1880s by a group of ardent Aesthetes—and that Oscar Wilde was an honorary member. Julien pursed his lips and gently nodded, suggesting the remote chance that the establishment may meet his approval, and returned his gaze to the passing countryside. When Asquith said this particular stretch was especially pretty if there was still enough light by which to see it, Julien said there was light, but that it did not come from the sun. His droll tone alerted his companions that something strange had entered his field of vision, and they both leaned towards the window.

What they saw was visible for just a passing moment, during which no one spoke, for at the top of a treeless knoll burned a bonfire surrounded by a group of dancing figures. Although they were several hundred yards away, two things were unmistakable: the figures were all women and children, and they were completely unclothed.

"Probably just druids," said Asquith, settling back in his seat.

"Never known druids to do anything like that," said Zoe apprehensively. "I mean, from what I've read..."

Asquith hired a coach at the station and the Americans reveled, wide-eyed, in the ride through the capital city of Albion to Berkeley Square. Julien stood before Poodle's Georgian edifice, took in all the street lamps, sounds, and smells and said to himself, "So this is

Londontown." In another life he would have enjoyed it, but now he just felt numb. The mystery of his father and the true identity he was forced to unravel hung about him more thickly than the city's famous fog.

Asquith and Zoe were whispering in the carriage, and Julien was told to go inside while the theatrical agent took her to Hotel Rosalind. Julien said he would message her there the following day. Zoe said good-night and blew him a kiss.

Julien settled into his room and arranged for roast beef, bread, and two bottles of claret to be brought up. When he was finally alone, he loosed a torrent of tears. His last remaining earthly possessions were gone; all he had were the clothes on his back and a billfold of notes that may or may not see him accomplish his task, which was still too fantastic to believe. When the claret arrived he downed it in gulps, and soon fell into a deep and dreamless sleep.

Heavy rain fell throughout the following day, and, with his mind already across the channel, Julien felt no desire to see Londontown. He wrote a note to Zoe and took it downstairs to be delivered, then returned to his room and waited for a reply, alternately dozing and staring out the window at the wet city. When the dinner hour arrived without any reply, Julien marched downstairs with the intention of skipping the meal and crossing the soaked city to check on Zoe.

He was met at the base of the stairs by Asquith and what he took for a fellow club member, before recognizing Zoe disguised charmingly but unconvincing as a young fop.

"You snore," she smirked.

"Why, you mischievous little..." Julien fumed. "What about the Hotel Rosalind?"

"No such thing," said Zoe. "Brush up on your Shakespeare!"

"Never cared for him," Julien scoffed.

"As you like it," quipped Asquith.

There was a pause as Julien released an exasperated sigh, then the trio broke out into hearty laughter.

Making their way to the dining room, Zoe explained that she had done her banking and was flush for the next leg of her journey, while Asquith told about how he had arranged a club member's private yacht to take them from Folkestone to Calais. Julien's appetite suffered an initial blow from the room's mauve decor, but the dozen gentlemen Asquith had invited to join them were a delight. Try as he might, Julien could find no fault with these genuine aesthetes. If their mannerisms were affected and their clothing flamboyant, they nonetheless earnestly recounted their youthful discoveries of the art of the Pre-Raphaelite brotherhood, the writings of Walter Pater, and the poetry of Swinburne.

"We understand you're a poet yourself," said one of beauty's acolytes. "Might you tantalize us with one of your confections?"

Julien sighed with feigned reluctance, which brought a round of applause as delicate as flapping butterfly wings, licked his lips, and intoned the following:

I like to write verses
In the backs of old hearses
And imagine dead cries and ghastly ghost curses

For to ride
At the side
Of one who's just died
Gives a life to my writing that can't be denied!

It's a portable room
Of deathly dark doom
A black cryptic carriage of clattering gloom

That's so warm and cozy
Just right to write poesy
(Though the formaldehyde makes my head feel quite dozy)

If someday I should claim
A bleak book to my name
You'll know right away whence my ideas came

For my grand inspiration
Comes from this deviation
And will bring me great fame, or eternal damnation

The lovers of beauty sat silently, eyes riveted on Julien, who stared back with a Mephistophelean grin before taking a sip of wine.

A moment later the room burst into laughter, causing Julien's grin to grow considerably. When Asquith said Julien was a composer as well, and Zoe added that he had the voice of an angel, the members demanded a performance. "Sing! Sing! Sing!" they chanted, pounding the table and causing the crystal and china to chime.

"Very well, lads," Julien said, rising from the table like a king. "Take me to thine pianoforte!"

The aesthetes roared like hearties on the rugby field, marching Julien out of the dining room and into the parlor, where every dandy, rake, and jaded sophisticate in Londontown had assembled to behold the macabre troubadour from America, swarming around him like a pack of lilac-scented peacocks.

Julien took a seat at the gilded Rococo piano, which harmonized perfectly with the turquoise-colored parlor. With heavy curtains behind him and the white sheer panels fluttering faintly from the outside breeze, Julien commenced a series of arpeggios in the key of F sharp minor. When the impromptu was complete, he let the last chord linger and then, into the waiting silence, unsheathed his voice:

Darkness is my hobby
  Black's my favorite hue
My mind's a hotel lobby
  Of characters to view

I shun the rays of light
  Can't bear to let them in
My bedroom shines so bright
  From the inferno of my sin

I cut my meat with swords
  Drink wine from Grecian vases

I'm falling swiftly towards
Some low, forbidden places

I read Baudelaire all night
Licorice is my favorite flavor
I shun everything that's white
Only ebony can I savor

Finally in his element with a proper audience, Julien was unprepared for what followed. The lilac-scented mob dragged him from the piano, petting his clothes and stroking his hair while shouting as though he were King Arthur and Merlin the Magician combined. Asquith grabbed hold of his arm to escort the sanctified singer to safety, where a man in evening dress sporting a green carnation stood applauding.

"You are truly an Adonis sprung from the underworld," the man said. "Heaven and Hell cease hostilities the moment you open your mouth."

Asquith proceeded to introduce Julien to Oscar Wilde. While the two artists shook hands, a motley merrymaker approached, wearing the mask of a golden youth with cherry lips.

"I adore your work, *The Soul of Man Under Socialism!*" exclaimed the masked man.

"Calm yourself, my dear boy," Wilde drily intoned, "it isn't *that* good."

"Oh, but it is! But you know what? I like *The Picture of Dorian Gray* even better!"

The man removed the waxen mask to reveal his own pus-oozing face. But his hallucinatory hideousness was overshadowed by something far more sinister, for in his other hand he raised a jagged blade and prepared to strike.

Once again a strange force took hold of Julien. The blade was aimed at the throat of Oscar Wilde, but Julien intercepted it, parrying the assassin's blow. In the ensuing struggle the dagger whisked like a comet across Julien's face before another parry sent it to the ground.

The motley assailant soon followed, falling to the floor under a hailstorm of Julien's fists.

Blood dripped from Julien's cheekbone as Asquith hastily dragged him, Wilde, and Zoe out the front door of Poodle's and into the rain-soaked night, where they trotted for half a block before hailing a hansom cab, destination Victoria Station.

"I'm afraid our members simply aren't vetted the way they used to be," Wilde quipped when the ordeal was behind them. "Cut me and you deface an artist, but cut Mr. Stanwyck and you deface art itself."

"You are too kind," Julien said, wiping his cheek. "But I'd add that the only thing worse than surviving an assassination attempt…"

"… Is not surviving it," said Wilde. "And I shall use that line when the gentlemen of the press come around."

"What the devil has gotten into people lately?" said Asquith, nerves frazzled.

"Perhaps the Devil himself," suggested Wilde.

The celebrated wit stayed with the trio until they reached the station, where he reluctantly bid Julien a fond farewell. "You have the two greatest things in the world in abundance, Mr. Stanwyck: youth and beauty. May they guide you to your destiny, which I've no doubt will be glorious."

Soon the three travelers were on the train to Folkestone. But when they reached the ancient town wedged between two cliffs, Asquith began leading them towards a dilapidated steamer berthed in the harbor.

"I know a thing or two about yachts," said Zoe with suspicion, "and that's no yacht."

"It's the midnight ferry," said Asquith matter-of-factly, "and we'd best get on it now."

"You lied to us?"

"I had to," Asquith confessed irritably. "That was ages ago, before dinner, before the performance—before the assassin. I had to say something to tag along."

"Tag along?" Julien inquired.

Asquith rhapsodized his plans for the singer, who shook his head in disgust. With no alternative but to take the ferry, Julien escorted Zoe down the dock before suddenly halting. Rummaging through his coat, he announced his billfold was missing. Zoe tried to console him, but he pushed her aside, seizing Asquith by the lapels.

"It was that mob at your club!" Julien raged. "Did you plan this whole thing? Leaving me penniless?"

Frantically Asquith pleaded innocence, begging not to be thrown into the harbor. The ferry sounded its horn, and Zoe cried for Julien to let the man go.

"Paris is expensive!" Asquith shouted as they marched down the dock. "I'll make you rich!"

"I despise money," Julien sneered back, "and all those who traffic in it."

"Then I'll make you an aristocrat!"

Julien stopped. "What did you say?"

"An aristocrat. An Elegant. Gothic. Aristocrat."

"How?"

"Your music. Your voice. Your face."

"My face is ruined," Julien scoffed.

Zoe grabbed his chin and tilted his visage towards the moonlight. The bleeding had stopped, and across Julien's cheekbone, at an angle of Pythagorean precision, was a perfect scar.

"Your face is not ruined," she said in awe.

The horn sounded again and a porter shouted the last call.

"I had nothing to do with your billfold," Asquith said, straightening his coat. "And honestly, Mr. Stanwyck, the way things are going for you so far in the Old World, what have you got to lose?"

CHAPTER FOUR

FINDING THE door unlocked, Simon Asquith turned the knob and entered, catching his breath from the four flights of stairs. Gray light filled the spacious top-floor studio in the Latin Quarter, which was entirely empty save for a piano and a bed, where Julien Stanwyck lay beside a sleeping damsel.

Asquith cleared his throat.

Apologizing, Julien nudged his companion, climbed out of bed without a hint of modesty, and pulled on his trousers. Barefoot and shirtless, he led Asquith to the piano for their business meeting, plunking melodies while his impresario delivered the news.

"Have you nothing to say?" asked Asquith.

"I'm glad there's no audition."

"That's all thanks to a letter from Oscar calling you the greatest entertainment sensation he's ever seen. Julien, this is monumental."

"And I can play whatever I want?" Julien asked with a flourish across the keyboard.

"Chat Noir has given you *carte blanche,*" Asquith replied, glancing at the bottles of cognac on top of the piano and the tawny figure dressing herself. "Your debut is this Saturday, so I suggest you concentrate on preparing your material."

Continuing with other business matters, Asquith said he had tracked down Julien's legal contact; while the friend of Julien's late mother lived in Normandy, her son was residing in Paris.

"And he's a lawyer?" asked Julien, playing an indeterminate chord on the keys.

"His response on that matter was somewhat vague," replied Asquith. "Anyway, he said to meet him tomorrow at 11 at the Cemetery Café in Montparnasse."

Julien's companion, lithe and lovely as a doe, slinked across the studio, asking Julien to lace her corset.

"Well then," said Asquith awkwardly. "I'll leave you to your work. Oh, and you might want to consider a stage name. And I almost forgot: a letter from Zoe."

Julien dismissed the girl as if she were a chambermaid and grabbed the letter. After Asquith and the girl had left, he sat in the windowsill, broke the envelope's wax seal, and withdrew the letter inside.

Dear Julien:

I hope you've settled into suitable accommodations in the City of Light and that Mr. Asquith has succeeded in finding you an engagement.

I've only just arrived at Zapfe's castle, as its alpine location is more remote than I was led to believe. In fact, it's so difficult to find that only a chosen few ever visit, so I feel very privileged. There is a sense of kinship here unlike anything I thought possible. The place is truly magical.

I hope one day to show it to you.

Yours,

Zoe

Julien rose early the following morning, marking the end of his month-long sybaritic sabbatical. While he laughed self-deprecatingly at the cabaret engagement, he had to admit that his performance at Poodle's had brought a feeling he had never known.

He let his imagination wander through visions of accolades at Chat Noir while practicing the art of *flâneurie*, or strolling the boulevards of Paris, which, in the words of Francis I, was a universe all its own. A *flâneur* walked in a state of heightened receptivity, allowing his interest to be piqued by chance, with no particular destination in mind. Except that Julien had one, and when he arrived in Montparnasse with time to spare, he searched the legendary cemetery for the tomb of Charles Baudelaire, upon which he placed a single flower.

But while paying his respects to the poet of modern melancholy, the misty morning played a trick on Julien's eyes, and he thought he saw an apparition hovering beside him. He left the gravesite and walked along the Rue Froidevaux until he found a sign reading, "The Cemetery Café: Where It's Always Dead." Naturally, the establishment was packed.

A young man, who had no trouble recognizing the brooding long-haired American, waved him over. With his neat haircut and spectacles, Maurice LeBlanc gave off a decidedly intellectual air, looking every bit the man of the law Julien expected. Sensing that something was amiss, he inquired as to whether Julien was feeling alright.

"I visited Baudelaire's grave," said Julien, "and now these lines keep running through my mind, but I don't recall ever memorizing them":

On the pillow of evil sits Satan Trismegist
Who constantly lulls our enchanted souls
And the rich metal of our volition
Is wholly vaporized by this crafty chemist

It is the Devil who holds the strings that move us!
In repugnant things we find delight
Each day we descend deeper into Hell
Without fear, through a reeking darkness

LeBlanc said that the mind was a strange thing, highly sensitive to outside influences. He also knew the reason for Julien's voyage to the Old World, but said it would take time to find out whether he could rightfully claim the Comte de la Tour-Abolie's title and estate. "The kingdom has turned quite bureaucratic as of late," he said before taking a sip of espresso.

"You studied the law?"

"Yes, but I'm not an attorney."

Julien stared at him blankly.

LeBlanc explained that he had not taken his degree and therefore had no license to practice. The unexplained phenomena had led him to pursue other interests: chiefly, meeting with a group of occult initiates — Josephin Peladan, Papus, Stanislas de Guaita — at a place called Bailly's Bookshop. "All of us feel called to the ancient doctrines, the forgotten wisdom from before Voltaire, revolution, and industry. But my real love is music; I understand you play the piano?"

"When night has fallen and my phantoms come out," said Julien coldly, having lost confidence that the man would be of much use.

"Never played with anything as Romantic as a phantom," countered LeBlanc with droll humor, "but if I were to do so, now would be the time. I have a trio; we play the work of d'Indy, Lekeu, and Chausson at various salons."

"I have an engagement at Chat Noir," Julien said offhandedly.

LeBlanc was impressed and said he was eager to attend. Finishing his espresso, he assured Julien that he was on good terms with his former professors and would look into the case, but that Julien should neither get his hopes up nor put forth much effort before inspecting the property.

"Why do you say that?" Julien inquired.

"Most of our old castles have fallen into ruin," said LeBlanc. "The caste system is working through its involutive cycle, if you'll pardon the occult pretension. All the energy is with the bourgeoisie, upkeep of noble estates is costly, and the descendants no longer care. In New York you raise new buildings. Here we raze old ones."

When Julien confessed to not having even looked at a map, LeBlanc offered to accompany him to the estate. Tour-Abolie was a small village west of Paris; the train would get them close, but from there the best option would likely be horseback. Seeing that the man was of use after all, Julien accepted the offer, and LeBlanc promised to make arrangements for Saturday afternoon.

"My engagement is that evening," said Julien, "but not until midnight."

"Strange hour for a performance."

"Strange times."

Julien spent the rest of the week in a state of lassitude, his carnal thirst slaked. When Saturday finally came he met LeBlanc at the station, whose Art Nouveau sign, he laughed, was the most beautiful train-station sign he had ever seen. At the westernmost stop the pair disembarked and walked until suburb became countryside and countryside became village. The proprietors of the town tavern were a Monsieur Reynard, he of bulbous nose and ruddy cheeks, and his plump and pleasant wife. LeBlanc had arranged the use of two old stallions — white for himself, black for Julien — to take them across a valley and up a hill to the castle of the deceased count.

As the horses accelerated into a gallop, Julien finally understood why he had refused a haircut since the age of 14. Everything came alive as his locks flowed behind him, and he felt as though he had entered a fairytale — albeit a very dark one. LeBlanc rode with aplomb, and Julien, who had always considered himself a misanthrope, felt fortunate to have a companion, even if he hardly knew the man.

And then the page turned in the fairytale, as there appeared in Julien's vision a grand château, filling him with that indescribable feeling of eeriness the people of Gaul call *déjà vu*. The men dismounted and tied the horses at the front of the estate, which faced Paris. Finding the doors locked, they explored the property, discovering on the northwest side a withered garden leading to a dense forest, and an august tower standing sentinel above an empty fountain.

LeBlanc said that the old tower dated from the 1400s—hence the name of the château and village—and that the rest had been built later, still keeping with the Gothic style. A weathered rear door to the castle was ajar, beckoning them to enter. With LeBlanc following politely and silently behind, Julien investigated each part of the ground floor, passing through a kitchen, servants' quarters, library, *salle d'armes*, and spacious rooms whose function he could not fathom, all of which featured the same tall windows and piles of broken glass. Next he walked the winding stairs to the second floor, quickly losing count of the bedrooms.

When the pair returned to where they'd started—a great hall with vaulted ceiling—they could only stare at each other in disbelief, for if there had been ancestral portraits and antique furniture, deer heads on the walls and rugs on the floor, coats of arms and candelabra and everything else that had filled Julien's imagination, it was all gone. Nothing remained in the Château de la Tour-Abolie but an ornate piano bolted to the floor.

"The Pharaoh's tomb has been looted," Julien laughed mordantly. "The bastard got what he deserved."

"Why do you call your father a bastard?" asked LeBlanc.

"You're right," said Julien, sitting at the cobweb-covered piano. "*I'm* the bastard." He pressed his hands down and played an aggravated E minor tetra-chord three times at *molto fortissimo.*

LeBlanc found the harmony interesting and asked him to play it again, whereupon Julien voiced an E octave in his left hand and E F# G A in his right.

"There's great tension in that chord," said LeBlanc. "Might you play me some of your music? Perhaps what you intend to play tonight?"

Outside the sun was beginning to set through the broken windows, inspiring Julien to draw further tones from the ancient instrument. Then he let loose his voice, smiling with a touch of madness at hearing it echo off the stone walls. After one verse he abruptly stopped with feigned *ennui*, saying that it simply repeats itself.

LeBlanc, clarifying the chords — Am Dm Bm7b5 and G#m6 — asked if he might try, and began playing with great delicacy.

Julien had never heard his music played by someone else before, and a feeling of freedom led him to dance about the hall like a phantom. He climbed the crumbling staircase, stopping halfway up to belt out another verse. Mesmerized by the spontaneous showmanship, LeBlanc felt a strange, celestial force take control of his hands as a new and daring art form began to take shape.

From the second-floor balustrade, Julien spread his arms like a troubled troubadour to serenade the court below, which he envisioned filled with knights and princesses whose land was under siege. Then, as if transformed into a dextrous feline, he bounded downstairs and leapt on the sill of a tall, broken window. With the twilight illuminating him from behind, making him appear ghostly and numinous, he sang the final verse and disappeared out of sight.

"That was fun," he said when he returned through the doorway.

"Fun?" replied LeBlanc. "What's that?"

The men shared a hearty laugh, and Julien felt the kindling of the first real friendship he had ever known.

"You should prowl around stage like that," said Maurice LeBlanc. "A cabaret expects something sensational, especially a place like Chat Noir."

Julien asked whether he would be willing to play, and the young man said he would be honored.

Julien clapped his hands, filled with creative energy. "OK, after the last verse and before the final chord, I like to throw in the Devil's Interval. I do it like this."

At the sound of the infamous chord of dissonance, the ancient instrument let out a metallic clang as though a latch had been released. The men eyed each other with curiosity, then raised the top to reveal the harpsichord inside. They investigated until Maurice said "a-ha" after seeing something any piano-tuner would say did not belong there.

Stashed in the corner of the soundboard were three books and a letter tied together with a ribbon. Maurice removed the bundle and read the writing on the envelope, whereupon his eyes grew as wide as his glasses. He showed it to Julien, who, upon seeing his own name written in jet-black ink, turned as pale as a cadaver. Maurice suggested they return the horses and dine at the tavern, where Julien could inspect the items more comfortably.

Julien nodded and the men marched out the door, where they both detected a peculiar odor emanating from the dilapidated old tower.

When they reached the tavern they sat at a splintered table by the fire and ordered pheasant, bread, and wine. When their bellies were full and the bottle empty, Julien heaved a sigh as agitated as the tetrachord he had played in the ruined castle, and untied the ribbon holding the bundle of books.

The three tomes were an enigma: two obscure works of science and a privately printed edition of Baudelaire's *Les Fleurs du Mal.* When he broke the seal on the envelope bearing his name, Maurice excused himself to settle their bill and give Julien some privacy.

Julien turned the letter towards the fire light and read the elegant penmanship:

Dearest Son:

I have followed your development as best I could through the rare occasions your mother deigned to answer one of my missives. Every few years, if there was no response from her, I had an investigator in New York provide an update, following you to boarding school, university, and your cafe life. He's good at what he does, and that is how I know of your music and your signature use of the Devil's Interval.

Please understand that despite whatever your mother may have told you, I did not take her against her will. My will too was taken. Let me explain.

One evening during a fierce thunderstorm, her theatrical troupe knocked on the castle door. One of their coaches had broken a wheel while passing through the village, and as there were not sufficient accommodations, they hiked here seeking food and shelter.

At midnight an occult force brought your mother to my chamber, not me to hers. Gothic blood flows in my veins, and I believe it was a consanguinity of the blood that brought your mother and me together that night and resulted in you.

If you're reading this, it means an evil has sprouted across Europa and claimed me as well. It is a kind of spiritual sickness, deeply sinister, and capable of assuming infinite guises.

Find and fulfill your destiny, my son, which I'm sure is intimately entwined with the fate of our race.

May we meet someday in the Astral Light.

Your Loving Father,

Cmte de la T-A

Post script: I'm sure Zapfe will find you somehow. His powers are great, and you should trust him.

Julien folded the letter, placed it back in the envelope, and stared at the crackling logs. He remembered the name Zapfe—he remembered even better the girl who had uttered it. Then Maurice returned with the proprietress, who pronounced the late count a kind and gentle man, showing a pendant he'd given her, depicting the Sun and Moon, which dangled in the midst of her plump bosom. Maurice asked if she knew how he had died.

"The strange happenings you've heard of," said Madame Reynard, "many say it all began here in Tour-Abolie. Villagers could smell an evil influence in the air they breathed. I believe malevolent spirits took the count, along with his books and everything else. His passing has been a terrible blow. Most of the families who have farmed these lands for generations have all gone away.

"By the way, monsieur," Madame Reynard added, staring at Julien, "your eyes... Topaz. Same as your father's. I'm sure there's a noble spirit behind them, and may you bring fruitfulness to our village."

Julien faintly smiled as Maurice glanced at a grandfather clock standing across the tavern. "Good lord, Julien, we'll never catch our train!"

"It's not important," said Julien, still gazing into the fire.

Maurice would have none of it: this was the man's debut at Chat Noir. He arranged to use the Reynards' horses to get them all the way to Paris, handing over all the money he had. Julien secured the books in the saddlebag, and soon he and Maurice were galloping at full speed beneath the moonlight.

But hardly had they left the village when Maurice shouted a warning. Directly in their path was a glowing miasma, a green fog alive with primordial intelligence. Spooked, the horses emitted loud snorts and threw their riders. Before they could run, the miasma encircled Julien and Maurice, filling their lungs with fumes and sending them into a deep sleep. Eighty-eight minutes went by — the same number as keys on a piano — before they awoke.

The horses were grazing in a nearby field, and when Maurice returned with them he said it was past 11. But the green sleep had awakened something in Julien, who had already survived a maritime disaster and stopped a murder. If a dark shadow were following him through the Old World, he was determined to defy it. The men raced through the darkness until the City of Light appeared, followed by the sounds of carriages, and finally the nocturnal wanderers' voices as they entered the heart of the city. When they reached Montmartre, Maurice took a detour he said would take but a moment.

Julien arrived at Chat Noir to find Asquith standing alone on the sidewalk, smoking a cigarette. At the sight of Julien arriving dusty, disheveled, and, stranger still, on horseback, the impresario shook his head. "Do you have any idea what it took to get this engagement?" he growled.

"That sounds like a rhetorical question," replied Julien, tying the horse to a streetlamp. After being informed that there were plenty of patrons still inside despite the late hour, Julien began tidying his hair and clothing.

"What are you doing?" laughed Asquith. "The manager wants my head on a platter."

Then a carriage came clopping down the boulevard, echoing in the night, and Maurice climbed out with two men, one holding a violin case and the other a cello.

"Who the bloody hell is this?" Asquith huffed.

"No idea," said Julien. "Who the bloody hell is this?" he queried, mocking Asquith's plummy accent.

Maurice introduced himself as Julien's new musical director, along with Charles and Pierre.

"Julien, the show is over!" exclaimed Asquith.

"The show is not over," said Julien, throwing open the door of Chat Noir.

"You can't!" Asquith shouted, chasing after him. "You'll never! For one thing, you look terrible!"

Julien removed his coat and threw it over his head as he marched into the bowels of the cabaret, which was filled with a patchouli-scented potpourri of bohemia and *beau monde.*

"Your face! Your hair! You're filthy!"

Julien tore off his shirt and the crowd watched as the skeletal young man strode across the room, grabbing a glass from each table he passed and, to the annoyance of the patron who had been enjoying the libation, proceeded to pour it over himself. Dripping brandy and champagne, he stood on the stage and stared into the crowd of Chat Noir like a panther set on devouring them.

As Asquith frantically calmed the manager, Maurice sat at the piano and clarified the chords to his fellow musicians. Julien sank to the floor and curled into a ball, and the room became as silent as a church on Sunday.

Asquith bounded onto the stage, where he was stopped by Maurice, who whispered to the impresario. Asquith pursed his lips as if to say, "Not bad," and announced to the audience, "*Mesdames et Messieurs*, allow me to present Count Wrathchild And The Castle Ruins."

Maurice set the tempo with a baroque flourish. Charles the cellist caught on first and began strumming deep bass notes, and soon Pierre was adding chilling phrases on the violin. When the introduction was complete, Julien rose to his knees as though he had been reanimated by a necromancer and sang his poetry:

Picture, phrase, distortion and lie
Feed like a virus upon us each day
Molding our souls that wait passive like clay
And filling them with lust for things to buy

In newspaper pages we watch our friends drown
A thousand lies sweep them to sea
Unable to tell fiction from reality
They slip into sleep without emitting a sound

Industry displays its toys like the legs of whores
Using tempting words that mock our minds
While the promise of pleasure quickly blinds
Us to the poison washed upon our intimate shores

If these seductive arts in which we so excel,
This whirling hurly-burly crafted by loons
Has found its way into my mournful tunes,
Then I, too, have drowned in the swell

But if the crown of progress we complacently wear
Has yet to corrupt my youthful sincerity
Then I shall sing of myself with no mercy
And leave rotten society to the poets who care

Artificial pleasures lead to natural pain
Such is the fate of the future clan

My fate as well; I'm a 20th-century man
And spew out of spite this spittle from my brain

When the song reached its climax and the Castle Ruins summoned the Devil's Interval, Julien stood with his head thrown back and eyes closed, his dripping ribcage heaving beneath the wet hair that clung to his frame.

The next thing he knew he was drying himself off with a towel while rummaging through bottles of ladies' perfume on the dressing-room's vanity table when Maurice, Asquith, and the cabaret's manager came bursting in.

"How did you do that?" Asquith asked in a state of shock.

"Did they like it?" said Julien, spritzing himself with *eau de toilette.*

Asquith recounted how one moment Julien had been standing there and disappeared the next.

The manager, equally perplexed, explained that there was no trap door on the stage. "We are not a theater that deals in silly illusions. By the way, bravo monsieur!"

"What the devil are you gentlemen talking about?" Julien laughed. "I simply left the stage and came back here. This is lovely, by the way. May I have this?"

"*Incroyable!*" a harried waiter said at the dressing-room door. "I've never seen anything like it! They demand an encore!"

"Well?" Asquith barked. "What are you waiting for?"

"Wait," the manager said craftily. "Tell them to come back tomorrow night."

He and Asquith exchanged glances like two men seeing gold in each other's eyes.

"Yes," said the impresario. "And every night thereafter."

CHAPTER FIVE

"RE YOU SURE he's expecting us?" asked Maurice LeBlanc after knocking.

"He said four o'clock," replied Simon Asquith.

"Knowing Julien," said Maurice, opening the door, "he probably meant 4 am. Hello?"

"*Entré*!" replied a suave baritone.

Accompanied by a lady of austere fashion, the pianist and impresario entered and proceeded to seek the singer in the once-empty studio, which had been transformed into a maze of Japanese screens in black lacquer, with acres of navy muslin cascading from the ceiling. The trio followed Julien's voice, treading over the Russian black bearskins that covered the floor and passing through a heady fog of opium incense before reaching the studio's far side, feeling as though they had just navigated a Byzantine palace. They found Julien backlit by the afternoon sun — which asserted itself as much as it could through the thick curtains of violet velvet — sitting at an eating area comprised of a black and gold table in the style of Louis XV, with matching chairs upholstered in leopard.

Julien sat wearing velvet slippers with Count Wrathchild crest, black satin breeches, and a tiger-print robe. As this was a business meeting he was naturally shirtless, and bid his guests to sit down with a wave of his ring-encrusted hand.

"Really, Julien," said Simon, "I think it's time you moved to a more fashionable faubourg, especially if you're to entertain guests as distinguished as the Duchesse de la Fontaine-Sombre."

"A title like that deserves three kisses," said Julien, pressing his lips to her gloved hand.

"*Enchantée*," the lady said in a conspicuously American accent. "And please, call me Regina. I'm sure we met in New York. I was Regina Grossman back then."

"Ms. Grossman, or rather the duchess," Simon corrected himself, "has not only sat for Boldini and Helleu, she's the heiress of one of your great American dynasties."

"Is that so?" said Julien.

"My father was in factories," Regina said offhandedly.

"And whatever are you doing in Paris?" asked Julien, snapping his fingers in an effort to summon some unseen servant.

"We'll get to that in a moment," said Simon. "First, there's much news to discuss."

"Then let us pow-wow over tea and cakes," Julien said, elevating the urgency of his snapping fingers to clapping hands.

"And here I was, expecting Transylvanian wine in skull goblets," Regina quipped.

Julien drew his fingers to his mouth and let forth a loud whistle. Soon afterward three young ladies came giggling through the labyrinth bearing trays. Part of Julien's revolving retinue of *demimondaines* known as "wrathvixens," they were clad in satin bustiers, stockings of lace and boots of suede, and wearing bottoms whose back consisted solely of a thin strip of fabric buried in the folds of their posteriors.

"They certainly look delicious," said Regina, eyeing the trio of derrieres before taking one of the cakes.

The tea was the finest from Ceylon, Julien boasted, and the cakes were made with a rare Indian spice said to be an aphrodisiac. "Which means the Duke of Dark-Fountain might find himself a lucky man tonight," he winked.

Regina said alas the duke's luck had run out several years ago, when he drank from their dark fountain and promptly expired. When Julien expressed his condolences, Regina explained that she had grown accustomed to widowhood, given that he was husband number three.

"With that title of yours," said Julien in an effort to lighten the tone, "you should join our little coven."

"Funny you should say that," interjected Simon. "But before we discuss the future, let's close the books on the past. I've finalized exit negotiations with Chat Noir, Julien, and your obligations are considered fulfilled. It's been an incredible year, and now we're on to the biggest stages in Europa — opera houses, royal theaters — each sure to be sold-out, from Copenhagen to Saint Petersburg."

"How exciting!" Regina exclaimed with applause.

Julien bowed his head in mock modesty, and Simon said he would next turn matters over to Julien's legal counsel.

Maurice slapped his hands on the table in a case-closed gesture of triumph, saying that he had received a letter just that morning. "The château is yours, Julien. You are officially the Comte de la Tour-Abolie."

Regina applauded even more assiduously, and Simon said Julien certainly had no choice now but to move to these vastly more fashionable accommodations — where there would be plenty of room for himself.

"But it's so far from town..." Julien yawned, "and the cost of upkeep... isn't that why the castles are all crumbling?"

His guests looked at each other before turning their gazes back to Julien. Simon explained that Regina was prepared to finance the restoration of the château, causing Julien to laugh skeptically.

"Oh, but I have all the right connections," Regina assured him. "I've done this before, you see, and right next door. I'm your neighbor. We share the same forest."

"Don't let me catch you poaching," said Julien playfully, lighting a cigar.

Simon silenced the levity, saying the duchess was on the cusp of unveiling an enterprise that would make for a splendid partnership. Regina had taken her father's *savoir-faire* in the factory trade and discovered a novel way of distilling absinthe.

"It has all the sweetness you could want, thanks to our proprietary wormwood," she said. "And we can make it twice as fast as our competitors at half the cost."

"And what, pray tell, do you plan to call this cheap, sweet concoction of yours?" Julien asked, flicking ash in his teacup.

Regina presented him with a green bottle bearing the name *Demos: The People's Absinthe*, featuring a Greek column surrounded by a swarm of green fairies. Julien smirked, saying that it would no doubt be a great success, but that he did not understand what it had to do with him.

"We'd love to introduce it to the marketplace at a grand fête, with you as the star attraction. Something that will be not just the talk of Paris, but the entire kingdom. A masquerade ball. At a castle."

"Yours?"

"No," Regina replied, "yours."

Julien laughed, dropping his cigar. "The castle of which I've been lord for all of ten minutes? That I visited once, a year ago? I don't live there. No one lives there. Actually, that's not true: spiders and rats live there."

Regina said that they only needed to refurbish the great hall, ballroom, and spruce up the entrance and gardens. "The state of desuetude only makes it more Romantic. Are you not the leader of the Castle Ruins?"

"I feel fatally wounded in our negotiations," said Julien, "by your use of the word 'desuetude.' And when are you thinking of throwing this *fête galante*?"

"April 30: *Walpurgisnacht*," said Regina. "Count Wrathchild's Walpurgis Night's Ball."

She placed a stack of papers on the table, which Julien ignored, asking if Simon had run the numbers.

The impresario said he had, and that they were quite attractive. "In the spirit of Walpurgis Night," he said, "you could almost call them black magic."

Julien released a long cloud of blue-gray smoke. "Then what the hell: bring on the black magic!"

The group erupted in celebration, whereupon Simon invited them all to dinner at Maxim's. Julien declined, however, saying he was a prisoner of the wrathvixens.

But his caresses that evening had not their usual ferocity, as Julien's jaded senses succumbed to thoughts of the château, the mystery of his father, and the Tarot spread on his fateful voyage across the sea. It was during the afterplay, as he drank aged cognac from a crystal snifter and directed the wrathvixens' writhings, that one withdrew her lips from another's loins and spoke in a tone of wounded vanity.

"What did you call me?" she chastised.

Julien said that he was quite certain he had called her many things, the naughty little strumpet.

"It's Chloe."

"Of course it is."

"You just called me Zoe."

Julien leapt up, gathered their dresses in his arms, and hurled them at the threesome, ordering them to leave immediately. When they protested, he roared in rage and set about rearranging his studio, systematically reducing it from an enchanting maze to site of the apocalypse.

When his spleen was purged of its bile and the wrathvixens had gone, Julien filled his alligator rucksack with the items he needed and set out into the night, stopping the first coach that passed and asking the driver to take him to La Tour-Abolie. When the coachman laughed and bid his horse walk on, Julien waved a handful of bills with an offer to buy the animal.

"She's not been under saddle since she was broken," the coachman replied. "But for a sum like that I can get you one."

Within half an hour Julien was galloping across Paris. Having had no desire to visit the estate while it stood in legal limbo, he now felt an overwhelming need to see it immediately, even if it meant riding like a madman through the night.

When he reached the village shortly before dawn, there was just enough moonlight to make his way across the valley and up the hill to the château. Julien dismounted, hitched the weary horse, and circled around the back, where the foul-smelling tower hovered over the empty fountain, and the door remained unlocked.

With a suitable stick snatched from the withered garden, Julien took a fine lace handkerchief, doused it with Regina's absinthe, and lit a match. Laughing at his ingenious illumination, Julien stepped across the threshold with the torch held high and walked to the lone object inside the empty castle: the cobweb-covered piano where his father had hidden the letter confirming his patrimony, along with the three mysterious books, which Julien proceeded to place atop the piano.

Julien kept the books on display at home beneath a bust of Byron he had found at a curiosity shop, so they had never been far from his mind. The volume of Baudelaire, his favorite poet, was eerie enough, but the works of science were utterly baffling. The first was called *Ion: An Investigation into the Power of Electricity* by a man named Ronald Carter, while the second was entitled *Pygmies: Quest for the Lost Little People*, by Gerald McClosky, Professor of Anthropology at Cambridge University.

Julien initially thought that his father had intended for him to read the books, but intuition soon nixed the notion and he began to think that they must contain some hidden message. He had scoured every page searching for any irregularities that might be strung together to reveal some cryptic message, but there had been neither a marking nor any missing pages suggesting a numbers puzzle. Now, after more fruitless ruminations inside the château, the very source of the mystery, Julien accepted that it was something he was not yet capable of unraveling.

He smiled, imagining how his surmise would elicit approval from Zoe Wingate, to whom he commenced to write a letter. Holding the torch in one hand and leaning against the piano, Julien penned the missive:

> *Zoe:*
>
> *Apologies for the long time between letters. I have finished my engagement at Chat Noir and find myself a man of comfortable means with unlimited future riches, exactly as Simon Asquith promised that fateful night on the harbor in Folkestone.*
>
> *Moreover, I write to you now from the Château de la Tour-Abolie, whose rightful lord I have become.*
>
> *Is my mission done? Was the cabaret simply a means to an end that is no longer necessary?*
>
> *I don't know now what I want, what is my will, and something inside says perhaps I'm not supposed to have a will, at least not in the old way.*
>
> *The Tarot spread you did for me on the ship was:*
>
> *Death*
>
> *The Priestess*
>
> *The Tower*
>
> *The Hermit*
>
> *The Lovers*
>
> *The Devil*

The Emperor

If the death was my mother's, the priestess was you, and the struck tower was our sunken ship, it seems the hermit is next. And so I await the appearance of this mysterious personage—wouldn't it be droll if it turned out to be me?

I'm sure you must be busy with your occult studies, as you indicated in your letter over the Winter Solstice, and so I'll bid you good night.

Yours,

Julien

Post script: There will be a masquerade ball here in six weeks' time. Hope you can come.

He arrived in the village and peered into the tavern window, where Madame Reynard was baking bread. Julien rapped his knuckles on the glass to get her attention, pointed at his brow, and mouthed the words "topaz eyes." The proprietress smiled and came around to the door, whereupon Julien said he owed her a horse. He also informed her, with sincere but awkward modesty, that he was now the Comte de la Tour-Abolie and *grand-seigneur* of the empty château.

Madame Reynard let out a cry of joy, kissed Julien on both cheeks, then abruptly apologized for covering him with flour. She made him a *petit déjeuner* of coffee, bread, and smoked bacon, which Julien ate at the rickety table by the fireplace. When he could not eat another bite, Julien asked the woman whether she recalled his father having any visitors.

Madame Reynard searched her memory, saying that towards the end she believed he had had a guest, and that the two would come down to dine every evening for a month. When Julien asked whether she would be able to recognize the man's name, Madame Reynard shook her head.

"Not even a name like… Zapfe?" Julien prodded.

"Not even a name as strange as that. But, now that I think about it, I do recall bits of their conversation. They used to mention the Alps. Yes, I'm quite sure of it."

His American upbringing suddenly troubled by doubt, Julien inquired whether they had meant the French or Swiss Alps. Madame Reynard laughed, pinched Julien's cheeks, and shook them as if he were her 10-year-old nephew.

Julien hiked through the morning and sat for two hours at the station, reading Baudelaire. Across the tracks, buzzards were pecking a dead man, but no one seemed bothered by it. When the train pulled into Paris, Julien did not even take a cabriolet, instead humbly walking home to the Latin Quarter and dropping the letter to Zoe along the way. His legitimate nobility had already kindled a desire to cease ostentatious indulgence in favor of aristocratic austerity, and when he reached his studio, before giving in to much-needed sleep, he put his apartment back in order, vowing never again to destroy his own home in a gratuitous display of rage.

Over the following month Julien made regular journeys to the château, where Regina's army of workers were busy rejuvenating the garden, replacing the windows, cleaning the grand hall, and decorating the ballroom. Regina prepared an upstairs bedroom for Julien where he could comfortably groom himself before his performance, and so that he could dramatically descend the staircase to commence the festivities. Whenever Julien told her she was being extravagant, Regina assured him everything had been properly budgeted. Simon oversaw the preparations, leaving Julien to concentrate on creating new material, which Maurice scored for an orchestra he had assembled.

One day, over lunch in The Tavern Of La Tour-Abolie—which had been spruced up for the Reynards and bore a new sign in Medieval lettering and a silhouette of the old tower—Regina presented the latest developments. While the château's ballroom could only fit 100 people, there was plenty of room in the grand hall as well as spillover into the gardens, and many visitors would want to see the old tower, where a Tour-Abolie "tour" guide would recount the estate's lurid history, embellished with poetic license. Julien would thus perform four sets throughout the evening, with the ballroom cleared between each set for the next grouping of guests. Regina had therefore capped attendance for the event at 380.

"And how did you arrive at that number?" wondered Julien.

"Since it's Walpurgis Night," she explained, "I thought we'd pay sly tribute to the year the Roman Empire adopted Christianity."

"And fell soon after," Julien said with a chug of wine.

Simon was allotted two dozen personal passes, which he planned to give to members of Poodle's club in Londontown, who were eager to demonstrate their dandyism in the Gallic kingdom and tell snobbish tales about how they had been present for Julien's first performance. "They remain your most devoted fanatics," he said, "that is, of the male sex."

"Then bring on the oodles of Poodles!" Julien said with verve, before remembering his vow of austerity.

Regina assumed Julien's guest list would include the most prized wrathvixens in his harem, but Julien waved his hand dismissively and said that he would present a list of Decadent authors and Symbolist painters. Count Robert de Montesquiou-Fezensac, who continued to deny that he was the inspiration for Des Esseintes in Huysmans' notorious novel, said that he would be honored to serve as the evening's master of ceremonies. The bat was the chosen symbol of this haughty Prince of Aesthetes, and he had been largely responsible for the success of Count Wrathchild at Chat Noir.

On Walpurgis Night, the privileged Parisian pilgrims lined the road from the station with a caravan of carriages, all magnetically drawn to see the man whom the press had called "The face, voice, and spirit of Decadence that has spread across Europa — for which he may or may not be responsible."

As tensions were high in an era when one could not tell fact from phantasm, many guests had turned recluse, and so Regina had engaged a host of damsels dressed as green fairies to greet the carriages with glasses of absinthe to soothe their high-strung nerves before the dark trek up the hill to the ancient castle.

As the hour of revelry approached, Julien was in his chamber, stretched out on a chaise lounge and submitting himself to being embalmed. Chloe, whom he had brought along as his personal assistant to make up for having called her by the wrong name, was massaging a balm of Egyptian myrrh into his torso when a knock came at the door.

Montesquiou, who adored playing games of incognito, came in sporting a dove gray masquerade mask in the shape of a bat, which he removed and smiled with a primping curl of his mustache. "Is Count Wrathchild prepared to receive an illustrious visitor of the highest order?"

"Oh Monty, you pompous preening prick," Julien said, pouring a snifter of cognac, "come in, my friend."

"I suggest you rise," Montesquiou said, "for I refer not to my humble self. Allow me to present His Imperial Majesty Louis XXII."

Three guards entered the room, standing at attention, followed by a personage of distinguished bearing who wore a golden mask.

Julien leapt from the chaise, spilling his cognac. "Your majesty," he stammered. "Forgive my…"

The king held up his hand to silence his subject. Removing his mask, he said that he was eager to witness the performance from the most talked-about artist of the times, assuring Julien that no one was the wiser concerning his identity—only the Comte de Montesquiou and the Duchesse de Fontaine-Sombre. "Her late husband and I were cousins," the king explained, "and when I received her cordial invitation, I could not refuse, especially given that you have rocked my kingdom with your art."

Julien said that he hoped the performance would suit his highness's taste, and bowed.

The king donned his mask and exited with the guards just as Maurice came into the room in a state of distress, bumping into the man who, unbeknownst to him, was his royal sovereign.

"Julien," he said, out of breath, "we have no orchestra."

"What the devil are you talking about?"

Maurice explained that no one had seen any of them save for three percussionists, who were understandably distraught by their missing colleagues.

Then Simon entered, calling the scene downstairs a madhouse. "All set to make history?" he asked excitedly.

"Since the day I was born," Julien said, twirling his locks in the mirror.

Asquith surveyed the despondent looks that hung on the faces of Chloe, Montesquiou and Maurice and, with a dyspeptic look of sudden financial insecurity, asked what the trouble was.

"I'm afraid the orchestra is more of a *petit ensemble*," Montesquiou sneered.

Simon was confused. Maurice explained that the musicians were nowhere to be found, with Montesquiou adding that there was a special guest who would be "royally disappointed" if the show did not go on.

Then Regina entered, saying that the natives were getting restless, and was quickly briefed on the situation. Julien told everyone to relax, saying that he and Maurice would simply improvise, just as they had done during their first visit to the castle. After the group nodded affirmation, Regina began the event, standing at the balustrade overlooking the grand hall to welcome the masqueraders on behalf of Demos Absinthe and introduce the Comte Robert de Montesquiou-Fezensac.

"*Mesdames et Messieurs*," Montesquiou said with pretensions of perfidy, as though he were a vampire, "One year ago, a lost soul from the New World found his way home, a prodigal son with the face of Adonis, the voice of an exalted angel, and the soul of a fallen one. He has captured the twilight of Europa like no other artist of our day, and so it is my honor to present, in the beautiful decrepitude of this castle where our ancestors fought and feasted together, the one and only Count Wrathchild!"

Bat-catchers crouched below the balustrade released a horde of flying vermin, which flew about the candles burning in the wrought-iron chandelier suspended above the great hall, eliciting screams of terror and delight. The processing percussionists banged out a funereal march on a single drum, a rusty iron bell, and a triangle. A dozen wrathvixens swung smoldering censers, while revolving cut-outs mounted to oil lamps projected the Demos Absinthe logo across the castle walls in green light.

Julien Stanwyck emerged, last in line, hands clawed as if carrying fireballs of primordial energy. As he descended the stairs he beheld the convulsing crowd, so elegant in its finery, so macabre in its masquerade. Three hundred and eighty ardent admirers had come to his regal home to hear his art—including the king himself—yet all Julien could feel as he turned the page in the fairy tale of his life was that the two most important people, his mother and Zoe, were not present.

When the procession reached the bottom of the stairs and began its march through the grand hall to the ballroom, the crowd sought to get closer to the poet-prophet, their Dionysian star of the dark night. The green fairies, who carried Demos bottles and glasses on silver platters, were knocked about, the sound of breaking glass producing strange harmonies with the clinks of the triangle. Footmen shouted that only patrons with tickets labeled "Group 1" were permitted to enter the ballroom, but they soon cowered at the mad mob of masqueraders.

Intended to hold a hundred, the ballroom was filled twice over, and everyone else still in the great hall pushed forward to get a glimpse of Count Wrathchild. Some ran out to climb the windows and peer inside, silhouetted by the moonlight. When the wrathvixens watched the footmen flee the escalating hysteria, they joined in flight, followed by the percussionists, until only Maurice remained, taking his place on stage at the piano with an expression of mystic ecstasy combined with unflinching resolve.

"Walpurgis Night!" Julien howled, removing his mink robe to reveal his embalmed torso, his cry met by a manic wail.

"Not long ago," he commenced, prowling the stage, "vengeful revolutionaries tried to send our aristocracy to the guillotine, but it was they who lost their heads! Our castles may be in ruins, but our blood still pulses, and our king still lives!"

"Long live the king!" the crowd roared.

"And now, for the tale of another sovereign," Julien said, running his hand through his chestnut locks, "who fell head over heels for a virgin princess, who in turn demanded the head of a prophet. Do you all know who I'm talking about?"

"Yes!"

"I said, do you all know who I'm talking about?"

"Yes!"

"Then say her name!"

"Salomé!"

Maurice began weaving a tapestry of serpentine rhythms while Julien writhed his hips, thrusting like a satyr, the tip of his tongue between his teeth, and commenced his *chanson*:

Salomé, you virgin-whore
Serenade me with your turgid limbs
I know you've come here just for me
To feed my soul's tainted whims

Let this pounding rhythm be your bed
As torchlight illuminates your sweat
And the musky smoke be my panting breath
Invading your hair, my writhing pet!

Your lovely face is cold as stone
Your castrating lust, a recompense
Behind your eyes you laugh at Herod
While you drown his every sense

Green fairies flutter all about
And squirm with you lasciviously
Together you become Medusa's hair
A twisting, serpentine orgy

But Salomé, if I were king,
For your art I wouldn't care
I'd rather have your dancer's legs
Flapping sweetly in the air

A moment more, near-nude nymph,
And you'll have what you desire
For John The Baptist's head is ripe
And Herod's got his loins on fire

The sound that followed was something from the depths of hell itself, as though the very hum of cosmic chaos were vibrating, pulling the entire castle into a violent abyss. The revelers set upon each other voraciously, and not only with fists, but with fingernails and teeth. Outside, the figures at the windows took on the posture of lower primates, shrieking and rattling the windowpanes as they watched the carnage unfold. Then, as abruptly as it had started, as though a spell had been broken by the mere snap of a finger, it stopped. Women, half-naked with their torn dresses, bolted into the night with handsful of each other's hair, while men shoved eyeballs back into sockets or nursed arms that dangled, broken and rubbery.

When only the sound of the rustling bats remained, Julien and Maurice, frozen in horror, stared at the ballroom floor, which had become a lake of broken glass, blood, and absinthe, in the center of which was a silver platter with a severed head.

Julien walked to the piano, causing Maurice to rise from the bench, pale and vacant-eyed. "Stay," Julien said, sitting beside his friend. "I've been working on something. Bit of a departure. You might call it a love song."

He sketched the melody, adding chords here and there, and Maurice began expanding the harmonic possibilities. The pair worked together until footsteps echoed through the empty castle.

Simon Asquith and Robert de Montesquiou entered the ballroom and praised the stars that the pair were alive. In vexation, they asked what they were doing.

"Working on new material," said Julien. "What were *you* doing?"

They explained that they had been hiding upstairs, and asked whether the two had seen Regina, to which reply came in the form of shaking heads.

With a look of nausea and handkerchief held over his mouth, Montesquiou walked on his toes across the green and crimson floor, shards of broken absinthe bottles crunching under his feet. When he reached the severed head, he raised its mask with the tip of his malacca cane, then, shrieking like a schoolgirl, announced, "It's the king!"

Three days later Julien was at the window in the chamber upstairs, drinking cognac from the bottle and watching the parade of gendarmes marching down the hill towards the village. Simon entered, saying that the latest count was 13 souls lost on his estate, dozens more clinging to their lives, and a hundred more still having glass removed from their flesh.

"You said you'd run the numbers," Julien intoned, staring blankly across the valley, "and they were black magic."

Simon heaved an agitated sigh. "It will be lawsuits forever, Julien. The authorities believe you cast some sort of spell with your music, inciting a riot that resulted in the king's assassination. And didn't you think they'd find out you were the sole survivor of the *Saint George* tragedy?"

"Not sole survivor," Julien corrected. "There was another."

Simon said that more than one newspaper had hailed him as a hero for maiming a hundred members of the upper class and killing the king, thereby paving the way for parliamentary democracy. When Julien protested that it was Regina's event, Simon said that, in the eyes of the law, the atrocity had occurred on his property, and that, as a duchess, she outranked him. "She has been a paragon of diplomacy and tact, by the way, especially in comforting the royal family."

He concluded by saying that Julien should turn himself over and pray for the legal system to prevail, just as Maurice and Montesquiou entered the room. Julien asked whether they trusted their justice system.

"I did once," replied Maurice. "Then times changed, and I traded law books for grimoires. Man's justice comes from society and depends on who's in charge; absolute justice comes from God."

"Yes, well there's more," Simon continued. "I'm afraid they've locked your bank account. I'll see what I can do from Londontown. I believed in you, Julien, I really did. But an evil has sprouted up that no one understands. Someone has to bear the blame, and what better boogeyman than Count Wrathchild? I'm sorry, but I'm also implicated in this, and they may try to hang me as well."

And then with a perfunctory bow Simon Asquith said goodbye and left.

"These republicans," said Montesquiou, "will not only freeze your bank account, but they will seize this château. And you will be both the greatest enemy and greatest ally of the future they envision, of universal suffrage, or suffering as I prefer to call it. If the ascendant forces, this money-grubbing rabble of American business — no offense, *mon ami* — are victorious, delicate souls such as ours will never be seen again. I fear we are the last of our kind."

Maurice LeBlanc put his hand on Julien's shoulder and said that he would make his way through the blockade while he still could and return home to Normandy. Julien said that he did not blame him, and that he had always known he was cursed.

"You're not cursed, Julien," said Maurice. "I don't know what you are, but you should flee, and right this moment."

"You can't take the road through the village, even to get away from Paris," Montesquiou strategized. "But if you exit the rear and go through the western forest, turning north when it gets flat, in about five kilometers you'll find a town called Darrieux. There you could hire a coachman to take you to Rouen. It'll be a long journey, but you'll be able to catch a train to the Kingdom of Belgium and on to Bruges."

"Why Bruges?" asked Julien.

"Because nobody's there," explained Montesquiou. "Except Rodenbach. I'll write to him post-haste."

As Maurice voiced his approval of the plan, Montesquiou alerted those present that a convoy of gendarmes was on its way up the hill. Julien took a swig of cognac, threw on his coat, and grabbed his knapsack. The trio descended the staircase, crossed the grand hall, and exited through the rear into the afternoon sunlight.

Julien took three strides, abruptly stopped, and turned to lunge at Maurice. He threw his arms around him and planted a kiss on his cheek. "You've been the truest friend I've ever known," he said. "You, too, Monty," he added with a firm grasp of Robert's arm.

And then he was off, bounding through the garden, past the fetid odor of the old tower, and disappearing into the forest without so much as a glance over his shoulder at the castle which, for a brief moment, had been his. Now not only was he no longer the lord of the Ruined Tower, but Count Wrathchild was dead to the world. There was only Julien Stanwyck, embarking on a dark journey through the Old World, which would one day come to know his wrath.

CHAPTER SIX

THE CHURCH OF Our Lady was as quiet as the silent canals of Bruges. The sole sound was that of an organist practicing a piece by Franck with a single finger, filling the architectural masterpiece of the Medieval city with ethereal vibrations. Occasionally a holy man would pass through the empty church while Julien sat with his head bowed, inhaling a residue of incense many centuries in the making.

Then footsteps echoed through the church, followed by the sound of a person sitting down in the pew behind him. Over his shoulder Julien whispered the name of his contact, which the man confirmed, saying that he had come at great risk and could only spare a moment. Word of the king's assassination and Julien's fugitive status had spread through all the newspapers of Europa, with extensive descriptions of Julien's conspicuous appearance, along with a warning that he was an anarchist seeking to take down every monarchy on the continent.

"What is happening?" Julien asked the man.

"The tide of the European people has reached its peak and has begun to recede into the cosmic ocean," replied Rodenbach.

When Julien asked how to stop it, Rodenbach said that their enemy was neither a person nor a thing but a metaphysical force, and that if anyone knew the appropriate course of action, it was Zapfe.

"Who is this man Zapfe?" asked Julien.

"A magus of great power. He lives in a Hyperborean region. You could search forever and a day and never find his castle."

The organ grew silent and three monks near the altar began speaking in low tones, their eyes aimed at Julien. Rodenbach warned that Julien had likely been recognized, and when the fugitive asked his contact to convince them of his innocence, Rodenbach brushed the request off as futile. "They are of a priestly nature, devoted to their savior from Bethlehem, and cannot be trusted to defend Europa from the evil that has befallen her, for they have not your regal spirit."

"Then why did you choose to meet here?"

"Because it is a beautiful church," said Rodenbach. "But it is beautiful not because it is a church, but because it is Gothic."

He draped a hooded cloak over the back of Julien's pew, instructing him to wear it as a form of concealment. He also set down a sack of provisions, money, and the address of the someone else who could offer refuge: Edvard Munch in Norseland. Julien slipped on the cloak and gave Rodenbach a letter to Zoe, along with the forwarding address.

In Oslo the artist took Julien to a cafe, where he explained the vision in 1893 that had inspired him to paint his famous bridge-bound screamer. "I could already see twilight falling across the continent," said Munch, "and beheld a future in which society was no longer a living organism, but a collection of atomized individuals abandoned by heaven. They could no longer rely on the institutions they had created, which had turned against them as though demonically possessed. The response I saw to this existential situation was a terrified shriek, all the more horrifying because no one else could hear it."

Julien visited the fjords and spent time in snowy solitude until he felt the call to disappear once again. Munch suggested he cross

Scandinavia to Stockholm, and before Julien embarked a letter from Zoe arrived with sympathies for what had happened at the château. He replied:

Zoe:

I have become The Hermit of the Tarot, albeit of the fugitive kind. Write to me in care of August Strindberg in the Kingdom of Sverige, where I am now headed.

I neither feel like making music nor singing, but I wrote this sonnet for you, and offer it with my fondest wishes:

In the darkest year of my life, the end
of a long-tossing inner tempest,
of stumbling along through crook and bend
without a star to guide me from the forest,

I thought these sullen woods would ever be
my mournful home, full of dragons wise
in torment, but which I came with time to see
were mirages glimpsed through half-shut eyes.

And then, lo, there shone in the heavens an astral aide
to guide me from gloom with glorious beam,
and I came upon a church, where inside was a maid

whom I'd seen before as if in a dream,
with moon-washed skin and hair to blanket sorrow,
who spoke her name to me, and in doing so,

became real, though still like some damsel of yore,
and in my heart I felt open a long-closed door.

I hope to see you soon. Surely no one could find me in your mountain hideaway.

J.

In the Kingdom of Sverige Julien found the author having just published a novel titled *Inferno,* recounting his dark night of the soul. But

Strindberg had emerged from inner turmoil only to find the outer world in crisis. "My mind's eye has become obsessed with the breakdown of the family," he said. "The cancer that will ravage individual households in the century about to dawn will infect all of society. Moreover, making men and women interchangeable citizens under the doctrine of equality will only drive them farther apart, their irreconcilable differences exposed once they become competitors in the capitalist arena instead of mutually dependent partners in accordance with divine order. All culture will perish under these conditions."

Agreeing that Julien should stay on the run, Strindberg sent him to the painter Franz Von Stuck in the land of Germania. Hiding under his cloak and trying to be inconspicuous while he waited in train stations, Julien brooded over his morose tour of Europa. How majestic the Old World was, and yet Julien was forced to experience it in a constant state of fear, and all men spoke of was their sense of coming catastrophe. It was as if Julien were trapped inside some sort of Game That Must Be Played, and the name of the game was Decadence.

When he arrived in Munich he was given a letter informing him to meet the artist at Neuschwanstein in the Kingdom of Bavaria. There, in the most flamboyant castle ever extracted from the Gothic imagination, Julien was taken to the grotto where Ludwig II had dreamt away his kingship until 1886, when he walked into Lake Starnberg and never reemerged.

Julien found Von Stuck admiring the frescoes depicting scenes from Wagner's music-dramas, and the artificial pond on which floated the bark of the swan-knight Lohengrin. The artist greeted Julien by explaining that the white swan was an ancient Hyperborean symbol associated with Apollo, god of the sun and lord of their people.

"I keep hearing of Hyperborea," said Julien, after thanking the artist for giving him refuge. "Surely it was never real."

"Perhaps in primordial times," replied Von Stuck. "Now it simply endures as our spiritual wellspring, the place to which our race is returning after its long march through the annals of history. Do you know the philosopher Friedrich Nietzsche? He once wrote, 'Let's face it, we're Hyperboreans.' Somehow I know what he was trying to say. When a painting takes shape in my imagination, I feel I belong to forests and mountains and castles like this. But in my architecture, my creative work illuminated by the sun-god Apollo, I remain a neoclassicist. The Gothic and Grecian are but two streams flowing from the same Hyperborean fountain, inspirational forces of divine intelligence that live in eternity, in the infinite imagination of the Supreme Author."

Von Stuck said he'd write to D'Annunzio at his home in the Florentine hills, the Villa della Capponcina, adding that the Italian might know a place on Capri or Lampedusa where Julien could find safety and cease his wanderings. The men shared a carriage ride through the mountains to the train station in Füssen, where Julien scribbled a letter, asking Von Stuck to post it right away:

> *Zoe:*
>
> *I must see you. Everyone has been so kind in giving me sanctuary, but they want to make me an island castaway and I'd rather come to you in the Alps. For now, I'm off to Italia to meet the Superman Aesthete.*
>
> *Yours,*
>
> *J.*

The tall, long-haired troubadour from the New World, clad in leather and velvet, and the short, bald Latin *signore,* dressed in a beige suit and sporting a preposterous boutonniere, did not vibrate on a harmonious frequency. D'Annunzio commenced an immediate tour of his property, recounting tales of the Villa della Capponcina as if speaking of his own ancestors.

As Julien Stanwyck had lost his mother, survived a maritime disaster, foiled an assassin, become a cabaret star, won and lost a noble estate, and was presently wanted for the death of the King of Gaul, he struggled to contain his impatience at the poet's pontifications.

D'Annunzio sniffed every flower in his garden, pronounced its Latin name as if eating a bon-bon, rhapsodized about the exquisiteness of its scent, and concluded with a scrupulous account of the flower's rarity and cost. Julien pleaded fatigue from his travels and asked whether any letter had arrived. Indeed one had, replied D'Annunzio, whereupon Julien apologized and said that it was a matter of gravest importance that he read it immediately.

> *Dearest Julien:*
>
> *Do not come here. Go to Venezia. In that town, you will find a discreet pensione called Hotel Ulisse. We'll meet you there.*
>
> *Zoe*

It was the ideal excuse for a swift exit. As D'Annunzio summoned a carriage to take Julien to the station in Florence, he took the conversation in a different direction.

"All this talk of demonic possession spreading across Europa is just overwrought nerves," he opined. "That said, I have recently had a recurring dream. The Epicurean sense of life to which I've devoted myself since 1889 with my novel *Pleasure*—I'm sure you've read it—has completely disappeared. To dress with dignity, daydream in the sunshine with a book of poetry, watching the birds and clouds and feeling part of an ordered cosmos—no one in the dream understands these things. They no longer fantasize, and with this has come the death of voluptuousness, or lovemaking pursued as an art form. Everything we take for granted—champagne and pastilles, perfumes mixing with our animal scents, fabrics and fashions and the decorating of bedrooms to entice the senses, the dance of seduction—all that is gone. What remains is only bestial coupling, which the people in this world eventually come to regard with disgust."

Julien was repulsed by this diatribe and wished Signore D'Annunzio a swift end to such nighmares. But as he rolled through the Florentine hills, which were filled with fragrance and afternoon light, he meditated on his own erotic escapades and wondered whether he was a divinely inspired voluptuary or merely a crude beast. The cascade of memories rekindled his erotic appetite, and he vowed to head for the nearest brothel as soon as he reached Venezia.

But he left the Santa Lucia station only to discover the city wrapped in saturnine fog and pelted by rain. Clad in a black shroud, the gondolier was a caricature of Julien in his fugitive cloak as he rowed the visitor silently across the misty waters, filling Julien's mind with images of Charon ferrying him across the river Styx. It was the time of the Festival of Redentore, which celebrated the end of a deadly plague in the 16th century. But since a new kind of plague had come to the city, far more sinister for its invisible origins, the festival had been canceled. Accustomed to purging supernatural energies during that time of year, the locals had donned their carnival motley and went about their daily lives in the rain with their faces covered.

For three days Julien sat at the window of his room in the Hotel Ulisse, watching the downpour and masked wanderers, until finally there was a knock on the door and he was handed a letter.

Julien:

Come across the lagoon to the island of Poveglia. I'll be waiting beneath the tall tower at 6.

Z.

For the rest of the afternoon, Julien thought of just two things: the note was not written in Zoe's hand, and had been signed only with the letter "Z."

It was nearly 7 by the time he reached the small island in the Venetian lagoon, as he'd been forced to solicit six gondoliers before one finally agreed to ferry him. A mist fell in the twilight and there was not a soul around, but the tower was easy enough to spot. Julien walked past unlit buildings until he reached it, where he found a lone figure leaning against the tower with a large hat pulled over his head, concealing his face. It could only be one person.

"Where's Zoe?" asked Julien.

"In the Alps. Hard at work saving Europa. As we all are."

"Who the hell are you people?" demanded Julien, advancing closer.

"Once we stood at the center of our civilization," said the man known as Zapfe. "Then when the theater of action shifted from Hellas to Rome the people lost their way, the empire fell, and amid the ruins they embraced the story of the foreign savior. We preserved the Primordial Tradition through six centuries of the Dark Ages, and, in the Medieval period, persecuted by the church of the Hebrew god, we became known as The Order of the Sword and Rose. Now there is too much at stake for us to bother with what we are called."

Julien asked whether Zoe was ever coming to Venice, and Zapfe shook his head negatively. When Julien expressed the urge to strangle him then and there, Zapfe replied that then Julien would definitely never see Zoe again.

"Are you some kind of necromancer?" Julien shouted, grabbing Zapfe by the lapels. "Tell me what you've done with her!"

Unthreatened, Zapfe said that this was the very reason Julien had been chosen. He had courage and devotion, and would soon learn to control his rage and discover his dormant powers. Julien released his grip but continued to shine his piercing gaze upon the man, who suggested they get out of the rain, and that it was easier to simply show him the cosmic drama in which he was now involved. Zapfe led him to a nondescript building, where they descended a spiral staircase to a workshop filled with anonymous men tinkering with strange contraptions, who bowed their heads to the magus as he passed, and eyed Julien with curiosity and awe.

"What is this island?" asked Julien. "Why is no one here?"

Removing his hat to reveal his high brow and gray goatee, Zapfe explained that Poveglia was the most haunted place in all the world, and that Christian superstition had worked to their advantage. They had maintained a magical workshop there for two centuries, but now the time had come to face the crisis of the entire continent.

"To receive divine inspiration and create works of art," said Zapfe, offering Julien a seat at a workbench, "this is a noble thing and something we can do. To become initiated into the Mysteries, smelting vital energies to be reborn not as a human powered by spirit, but as a spirit in the form of a human — this *magnum opus* of alchemy is something we can do. To guard the flame of our ancestors, coalesced out of the ether at the top of the world in the land of Hyperborea, to preserve the wisdom of Atlantis and Hellas, when men and gods lived in communion and our race lived alone, untainted by the influence of others — whether as slaves, masters, or equals — to project images into the Astral Light and create magical chains in the minds of men — all this we can do."

"It sounds like you can do anything," said Julien wryly.

"Alas, we cannot. Zoe Wingate can see the Astral Light, which she often did from an early age without understanding her ability. In our alpine castle, and this workshop, we have assembled every kind of initiate with gifts like hers. We have alchemists, Neoplatonists, occultists, women gifted in clairvoyance, visionary artists — what we don't have, and have waited for so patiently, is a hero."

Julien scoffed, yet his body began to tingle.

The word "hero" comes from the Greek, meaning "protector" or "defender," Zapfe explained, and once referred to a man who had been forged by the divine science of the Royal Art. "Your stars signal the undertaking for which you are destined, which is the reason you have the stars in the first place. You have the face of a god and the voice of an angel, whose troubled art is that of a race facing extinction. You have the instincts of a warrior, the reflection of a philosopher, the soul of a poet, and the sensibility of a voluptuary — though obviously that will have to be sacrificed. There's only one man in the world with nothing to lose because he's already lost everything, whose mother sacrificed herself that her son might one day be king."

"Then I *am* cursed," said Julien, sick with confusion.

"In a certain way, yes. To be chosen is a kind of curse. Consider your lifelong obsession with aristocracy, the noble identity of your true father, your journey to the Old World, the chance meeting with Zoe, which was not chance but destiny. You acquired earthly nobility only to lose it, and stand now on the threshold of true acquired nobility, which is nothing less than conditioned immortality."

Julien begged him to stop, pleading that he was just a tormented artist, a court jester with a handsome face. But Zapfe said that in his ignorance Julien did not realize that his birth had been caused by things beyond his understanding.

"Did your father not say in his letter that an inexplicable force had caused him to make love with your mother, which her soul had already accepted, even though her human personality did not comprehend it?" Zapfe reasoned. "Have you not always dreamed of heroic epochs, despised the world of money and materialism, even as you reveled in its spoils? Stop resisting what you know to be true. Look at where you are: in a magical workshop in Venice, falsely accused of killing a royal, in a living nightmare of mass-hysteria. Your Tarot spread with Zoe was correct; we have all seen in the Astral Light that you have been not only called but chosen."

"But chosen for what?" Julien asked, his resistance faltering.

Zapfe sighed, paused, and said "theurgy." After receiving a befuddled look from Julien, he explained that it was from the Greek for divine workings.

"Meaning?"

"Meaning we need you to re-establish contact with the old gods," said Zapfe, explaining that Julien must go to Hellas, search the islands, find the slumbering gods of Olympus, and plead for their assistance. They would not give up on the land of Europa if a hero successfully found them.

"But how would I…? Where would I even…?"

Zapfe calmed Julien, asking whether he still possessed the books his father had left him. Julien opened his rucksack and lay them on the table, saying that he had wanted to destroy them a hundred times but could not bring himself to do it.

"Because you solved the riddle?" asked Zapfe.

"No," replied Julien, "because I could not."

"Then I shall help you," said Zapfe, "because you cannot embark until you have a heading and understand how the navigation system works."

"Navigation system?"

"Never mind that for now. The puzzle lies in the books' titles. Look beyond rationality, into the cosmic code of destiny."

Julien stared at the three books lying on the table:

- *Les Fleurs Du Mal* by Charles Baudelaire
- *Ion: An Investigation into the Power of Electricity* by Ronald Carter
- *Pygmies: Quest for the Lost Little People* by Gerald McClosky

Slowly Julien's vision began to separate the wheat from the chaff, the gross from the subtle, everything that wasn't David, as Michelangelo said, from the block of marble in which David lay imprisoned.

Pygmies: Quest for the Lost ….

…Les Fleurs du Mal…

…. Ion: An Investigation into the Power…

Zapfe watched closely as Julien continued meditating on the titles as if in trance:

Pygmies: Quest…

… du Mal…

… Ion: An Investigation…

"Yes," Zapfe said encouragingly, "You've almost got it…"

PYG*mies…*

du **MAL**

ION

"Pygmalion," Julien blurted out, breaking his trance. "Pygmalion? Is that it?"

Zapfe smiled, said that Julien would no longer be needing the books, and gave them to an attendant. "Books have a destiny of their own," he explained, "for they are filled with words, and words are a form of magic, which is why it is said that in the beginning was the Word. At some point the late Comte de la Tour-Abolie received the books, though I couldn't tell you how. He was unable to solve the riddle, but I did. Yet in the magical dimension where we perform our operations, we are often obliged to be as silent as the Sphinx. I did not reveal the answer, nor did I tell your father what to do with the books, because I understood that a higher intelligence was at work. It was he who devised the hiding place inside the piano, bolted to the floor, knowing that you, too, would one day come to the château and, in striking the Devil's Interval, release the latch."

When Julien protested that he still had no idea what Pygmalion meant, Zapfe said that the ways of the gods were mysterious and that man could only understand the sacred science of theurgy up to a point. Pygmalion was merely a heading; the navigation system would do the rest.

Zapfe snapped his fingers and an attendant handed him a cloth of purple and gold, which he unwrapped to reveal a large sea shell he called a magic compass. "This is believed to have belonged to the great Hermes Trismegistus himself, its origins going back through Hellas and Egypt, to the time before the Parthenon, before even the Great Pyramid. It was lost for centuries after the fall of Rome, but was returned to us by the Arabs, to whom we owe a debt of gratitude."

Julien took the shell in his hands and asked how it worked.

"Hermes, in his lower form, is known as the messenger god," explained Zapfe, "ruling over communication through the fast-moving planet Mercury, whose energy drives the miraculous creation known as human consciousness. Hermes is considered the bridge between heaven and earth, between the mortal part of man and his spirit. The vibrational frequency of consciousness where the divine realm begins—above the seven planetary metals corresponding to the seven visible astral bodies in the sky, which in turn correspond to the seven energy wheels, or clusters of intense nervous-system energy—is that of Neptune. This frequency rules the archetypal imagination. Can you say for certain where your music and poetry comes from?"

"No," replied Julien. "I've chased my muse my whole life and she always disappears."

"Neptune is the frequency at which she enters your mind and to which she returns," said Zapfe. "Common people never experience it, artists such as you channel it instinctively without understanding how, and initiates can summon it at will and control the images it produces. This is why the planet Neptune is said to be the god of the unseen world of the sea, and why Hermes Trismegistus owned this shell. This shell is a consecrated communication device between our world and the overworld, and is capable of passing through the Neptunian frequency to the Olympian realm. Do we not tell children that one can hear the roar of the sea when pressing a seashell to one's ear?"

Julien placed the shell to his ear and could hear the imaginary roar of the ocean, just as he had as a boy at school.

"The shell can also receive communications," Zapfe continued. "All you need to do is speak your intention and it will guide your way through divine magic."

But what Julien could not fathom was where they would find a captain willing to take him from island to island while he talked to a sea shell, without branding him a lunatic and throwing him overboard.

"Oh, no one can know what you're doing," said Zapfe. "Also, you won't exactly… well, you're probably not going to be on earth. We're not entirely sure, which is why we need a hero. Consider that when you sleep your body remains on earth, but you enter a different state of consciousness where dreams take place. Your mind experiences these dreams as real, and awakening from them is often a shock. It will probably be something like that, the ancient state of being called *mag*, from which we get the term magic. You slipped into it just now when you solved the riddle of Pygmalion."

Assuming he would even accept the mission, Julien could not understand whether he would actually be going to Hellas or just slipping into a trance and imagining it. Zapfe said that it would likely be a combination of both, that he would be crossing the Neptunian realm physically through the ocean, and metaphysically through its vibrational frequency in the Astral Light. "If our calculations are correct, you will enter a twilight realm of Being where gods and men once lived together in communion, a dimension outside of space and time because it lives in eternity, and this is where you will find Olympus. Now, let me show you what will take you to the threshold."

Zapfe wrapped the shell in the ancient cloth, placed it inside Julien's rucksack, and handed it to him with a nod. He crossed the workshop with Julien in tow, and the pair took a staircase down to a dank chamber where a short stone dock extended along an underground canal. To the right the water of the canal lapped against the gray stones, while to the left it led through a Gothic-shaped opening into a dark tunnel and out into the Venetian lagoon. Zapfe snapped his fingers once again, and a dozen attendants set to work amid the sound of cranking gears and jostling cables until the black water began to ripple, bubble, and finally yield up a fantastic brass-colored vessel some 20 feet long, which came to a rest, floating half-submerged on the surface of the water.

"Behold your submersible watercraft," said Zapfe. "Man spent centuries seeking to manifest it until Jules Verne, the author of the fantastic, birthed one from his imagination in 1869, calling it *The Nautilus.* A magical chain in the Astral Light was created by way of Verne's description and the illustrations that accompanied his book *20,000 Leagues Under The Sea.* By accessing this chain on the subtle plane we were able to glimpse the technics of the future, which we combined with our own divinely inspired images received through the Universal Plastic Medium. We have been working on this watercraft ever since, not knowing the hero who would eventually pilot it. Zoe gave the ship its name: the Scorpitaria."

Nauseated at the very sight of the ship, Julien said that the name meant nothing to him. Zapfe explained that it was a combination of "Scorpio" and "Sagittarius," and that it represented the Venus and Mercury placements in his birth chart—the stars that would help guide him, along with the sea shell of Hermes.

"Think back to your time with Zoe," expounded Zapfe. "Did she not guess you were born under the sign of Aries? And did she not also manage to pull the exact date from you? And later, in a completely separate conversation, did she not inquire whether you had been born in New York, not just raised there? From that she had nearly all she needed; the last detail was the time of your birth, which you yourself offered when you said that you took your first breath on the last stroke of midnight. Your sun is in Aries, ruled by the planet Mars, which governs action, assertion, and war. And you have it in the Fourth House, which represents history, heritage and home."

"I have no home," Julien said coldly.

"You're still thinking with your human intellect," countered Zapfe, "not the divine intelligence which is its root and source. The Fourth House only means home on the material plane. In the soul it is the very soul itself, and on the spiritual plane it is the realm of the kindred. You are not a lone fighter with no cause but himself, but rather a warrior called to defend his people. But there is so much more, for you have Neptune in the Fourth House as well. And when the Sun and Neptune are conjunct, you hear a cosmic music no one else can.

As for Venus and Mercury, they too are in the Fourth House, so your soul's true love is not the carnal appetite that rules you now, but the divine love to which it must be raised, for Neptune is the higher octave of Venus. Mercury brings your gift of poetry, the power that enables you to communicate the anguish of your soul and the crisis of your race, while the last and most important puzzle piece of your stars is the placement of the Moon. This governs the introverted and imaginative part of you, and represents the maternal influence. Your Moon is in the sign of Cancer, a sensitive and feminine sign, and both the sign and the planet account for your strong attachment to your mother, and your volatile emotions when this gentle Moon reflects your fiery Sun. Cancer is also the natural ruler of the Fourth House, further concentrating the story the Creator has written for you, in which the sphere of action shall take place within the realm of ancestry."

Julien pleaded for time to absorb everything, but Zapfe said that time was something they didn't have.

"You must know by direct intuitive perception," he said, "beyond all personal desires, hopes, and fears, that this is what you must do. You must do it right now, for Zoe."

"What do you mean for Zoe?" asked Julien with concern.

Zapfe explained that the past 18 months had been very hard on her. While she was extremely sensitive as a prophetess, in order to be of greater use in the cosmic confrontation unfolding it was necessary to undergo the process of alchemy. This was difficult enough for a man — many abandoned the process and went mad or died — but it was even harder for a woman. "Her entire being has to be repolarized from Mother Earth to Father Sky, to belong not to Life but to Being, not to vital energies but the Spirit that gives form to such energies through divine intelligence. I'm afraid she is trapped in the *putrefactio* state, and that's why we need the golden apple."

Julien was too overwhelmed to even react.

"The Apple of the Hesperides," Zapfe said. "Somewhere in Hellas. You'll find it. One will suffice. Unbitten, please."

Julien stared at the bronze-colored submersible. "You have no idea what I went through on that damned ocean liner," he sighed. "I'll die of claustrophobic hyperventilation before I reach Sardinia."

Zapfe burst out laughing, grabbed the iron step-handles on the side of the Scorpitaria, and climbed on top. With a scowl of trepidation, Julien followed to receive a lesson in how the ship was powered. Zapfe explained that sunlight was absorbed from the god Apollo through a kind of circulatory system of narrow pipes containing an amber fluid that fed the motor. Then Zapfe knelt and turned the handle on the hatch, showing how the interior was quite comfortable and suited to Julien's taste, with a leather seat and turndown desk for reading and writing, animal hides and cushions for sleeping on the vessel's floor, and images of Hellenic heroes painted on the walls between the portholes. "There's clothing, wine, water, figs, smoked meat… and see up there? That's the golden pedestal on which you place the navigation shell. There's also a philter with an elixir to calm your nerves when it submerges for the first time."

Julien marveled at the creation with awe and dread while, unbeknownst to him, Zapfe gestured to an assistant. Moments later there was a great deal of shouting and marching footsteps.

"Herr Zapfe!" a man shouted from across the dock. "The Chosen One must have been followed from the Lido. A dozen gondolas just landed on the island, filled with officers of the *Arma dei Carabinieri*!"

"What are they?" asked Julien tensely.

"Military police. You've got to hide."

Julien asked whether there was another way out, but Zapfe shook his head. Eyeing the canal, Julien said he would swim for it, but Zapfe said that it was too far and he would drown. All the attendants were running around the workshop in great distress, shouting that the police were barging through the door upstairs.

"Quick!" Zapfe said. "We'll submerge the vessel and hide you underwater. It's your only chance!"

Julien screamed in rage and climbed inside the Scorpitaria. Zapfe ordered him to place the sea shell on the pedestal by the aperture at the bow. Julien rushed astern.

"The other way!" shouted Zapfe. "Hurry, we can't stall them much longer. And we can't lower you until you put the shell on the pedestal and say, 'Take me to Pygmalion.'"

When Julien had done as he was told the amber pipes began to glow and the propulsion motor started to whirr. Zapfe slammed the hatch shut, turned the handle, and climbed off the ship as it began to submerge.

"It's making all kinds of noise!" Julien shouted through the porthole, the vessel already heading towards the opening leading to the lagoon.

"Julien," Zapfe replied from the dock with a stroke of his goatee, "I'd take that elixir now if I were you."

CHAPTER SEVEN

A LOUD THUD woke Julien from his sleep. As cognition came he noted that the Scorpitaria was no longer in motion. The dull whir — which had been a kind of nauseating low E flat that rumbled his entrails — had ceased. The amber glow of the vessel's circulatory system was dim, and pulsed gently as it recharged from the light of the sun shining through the portholes.

Julien had no sense of how long it had been. He remembered leaving Venice and the terrifying descent into the black waters, which caused him to down the philter, despite the distrust he felt for Zapfe. Then came a horrifying darkness, during which he saw his life pass before his eyes, but not as a detached spectacle. All his faults seemed to come alive, animated by some strange force with its own intelligence. He remembered screaming, turned inside-out against himself, attacked by his own living memories of selfish rage and philandering, cynical and predatory seductions culminating in the despotic harem sultan figure he had turned into, once having become Count Wrathchild, cabaret star and the talk of Paris.

Sex and violence, Julien thought as he drank water from the supply bin. *Creation and destruction, the two primary forces of human experience, birth and death, chapters that begin and chapters that end.*

As his mental acuity returned, Julien found himself feeling as though there were some sort of rot or black ice wedged deep inside of him that needed to be melted out. He scarcely knew whether he was in one of those strange states called lucid dreams, or whether he too had succumbed to the hallucinatory evil stalking Europa.

The portholes revealed blue ocean on the port side and a rocky cliff on the starboard side, which meant that Julien had arrived somewhere. He threw some bread and smoked meat into his rucksack along with a waterskin, then crossed the vessel and ordered the seashell to stay as if speaking to a dog. He turned the handle on the roof hatch, braced himself on the wall-mounted foot rail, and pulled himself on top of the vessel. The Scorpitaria had docked at the end of a jetty, which Julien crossed to the shore, then bounded up boulders to the top of the cliff, where he surveyed a flat countryside fragrant with oleander.

In the distance he could make out a dirt road. He approached it, discovering at its boundary a stone marker some five feet tall and carved with the face of a bearded figure. Halfway down the object two weather-worn testes and an erect phallus were visible. A subtle energy came into Julien, as though a breeze blowing through his hair, or a sudden inspiration for a song.

"Zoe..." Julien whispered to himself before halting his breath. "Zoe?"

"I'm here" came the vibratory response in his consciousness, situated somewhere beyond conventional language. "*Herm*," the vibration-voice continued, after which a flood of information spilled into Julien's mind. In an instant he understood that the marker was called a "herm," named for the god Hermes, whose many duties included ruling over journeys. In ancient Hellas herms were placed along roadways so that travelers could stroke the phallus, symbol of the generative principle of the cosmos.

He followed the road away from the coast until he could see buildings in the distance. Julien quickened his pace, and soon a row of trees framed the road, leading to a town of some kind. Julien's mind was struck by the story of Marathon and that great run beneath the Grecian sun. He ran hard, but when he got closer to the trees he halted his sprint, for this arboreal welcome party was made up of cypresses, the traditional tree of mourning.

As the road ended and he passed through a weed-covered gate, Julien found himself in a city both silent and deserted, the white marble and stone of the buildings having turned ash gray. "Necropolis," Julien received in his consciousness, again comprehending that it was Zoe helping him through the Astral Light. "City of the dead."

At the town center there was a square with a statue of Apollo standing atop a dry fountain. The fountain was surrounded by other statues with names on their pedestals, but which were nothing but skeletons. Julien had dreaded lessons in ancient Greek at boarding school, but his recollection was sufficient to decipher the name Calliope, muse of epic poetry, and Clio, muse of history. He counted nine skeleton statues, concluding that they represented the same number of Muses from Hellenic myth. Investigating the buildings around the square, he discovered broken pottery and a kiln in one of them; there were parchments turned to dust in another, suggestive of literature; finally he happened upon a completely empty building, which he took for a shrine to Terpsichore, muse of dance. Nine buildings faced the statue of Apollo, but not a single one of them had anything to do with the myth of Pygmalion.

"Where do I go?" Julien projected into the light.

In a flash he received a vibration, again as though a line of poetry or a musical melody had come to him from another dimension. Zoe's frequency helped him understand that in ancient Hellas there had been no muse of sculpture. But there was Hephaestus, the lord of crafts, among which were sword-making and the statuary art. Julien explored the silent necropolis, which fanned out from the center in the form of a spiral, and soon he came upon another skeletal statue, this one bearing the recognizably Latin letter "H." There were a handful of buildings nearby. After inspecting a smithy and a tannery, Julien entered a studio filled with marble blocks, chiseling tools, and an empty pedestal, before which stood a lectern scattered with tiles. He felt a deep resonance with the place, as though it were his fated destination. But with little more than tools and stone littering the environment, he could not imagine what he was expected to recover there.

Zoe's voice, like a melody running through the back of his mind, told him to be patient, and so he stepped forward to examine the lectern. The tiles bore letters of the Latin alphabet, arranged in such a way as to spell out a message:

ONLY THE HERO

"Only the hero..." Julien said to himself. "...Can do what?"

He stilled his mind and summoned all he could remember about the myth of Pygmalion and his love Galatea. The sculptor had dreamed of an ideal woman, created a representation of her, and asked the gods to bring her to life. Julien paused and pondered, then closed his eyes. Slowly he began to make out a harem parade, as one by one all the erotic conquests of his life marched by. A simple man would say that a philanderer of Julien's level could not possibly recollect a fraction of his dalliances, but such a man knows nothing of sexual obsession. Julien could remember the most exacting of details, recall his concubines' perfumes, ranging from sweet and floral to sultry and dank, the charms of their anatomy in its endless variety, the wantonness or reserve of their demeanors, their zeal, whether kept in check or unleashed, their gentle sighs and ecstatic cries.

Then something happened which Julien had never experienced before. Instead of cataloging the women like a mad collector of dolls, Julien watched them begin to lose their distinction, melting into one ultimate woman, revealing the cosmic force behind the frenzied desire they had inspired in him.

"Venus," Julien said to himself.

He now understood that behind each individual human woman he had known the divine power of feminine beauty had hidden itself, a combination of pulchritude and lubricity. For there could never be—at least for Julien—desire without beauty, or beauty without longing. Never before had Julien ceased his sordid chase long enough to realize that behind the Eternal Feminine, as Goethe put it, was a specific energetic vibration that ruled over its function in earthly life. In ancient Hellas that Morning Star, which poets called the fairest sight in nature, had been endowed with broader attributes and areas of rulership, and was known by the name of Aphrodite.

Julien opened his eyes and saw a half-invisible phantom glowing above the pedestal. He was unsure whether he was actually seeing it, or whether his senses had been distorted from dizziness. The energy-being possessed an electro-magnetic allure, like a fruit begging to be eaten or a fertile field wishing to be fecundated. Then he noticed something on the lectern that had not previously been there. Below the message were three extra tiles bearing the letters:

L E S

Julien recalled the Tarot spread he had drawn with Zoe aboard the *Saint George*, knowing now that something invisible had guided him to select those cards. From Zapfe he had learned that seeing beyond the rational world, while requiring an enormous leap in consciousness, became child's play if one tapped the proper frequency. Slowly and methodically Julien pulled tiles down from the message "ONLY THE HERO," slid the new tiles up, and adjusted them, revealing the message:

LONELY THE EROS

Julien then stepped back and beheld as the invisible vibration upon the pedestal began to solidify. At first light coalesced at its general location, concentrating into a space hardly bigger than a human heart before growing. It seemed to struggle through some kind of cosmic birth, being first ripped apart and then assembled, limbs sewn and stitched, painted and varnished, until there stood a life-size statue of a slender youth, his figure draped in a white tunic. Its substance was not that of marble but rather of a waxen consistency, and seemed as though all it needed to quicken was a spark.

"Behind the allure of woman is the longing for Aphrodite," said Julien as if reciting an incantation. "And behind Aphrodite is… Eros, born of primordial Chaos, binding force of the cosmos, operating between the material and immaterial, capable of uniting gods and men."

He opened his eyes, whereupon they were pierced by the gaze of the living statue.

"My what a dashing hero," said the youth. "Did you come by the left-hand path or the right? I say, are you a warrior or a poet? A fighter or a lover?"

Julien was speechless.

"Of course," said Eros, stepping down from the pedestal. "You are a courtier, a man for all seasons. You're the kind of hero who comes at the end, wielding the stylus of Pindar and the sword of Perseus."

Julien played along, saying that he had been sent from the earthly realm with only the name Pygmalion as his guide, but that it was clearly not he who stood before him. Eros said that the sculptor had joined the artists and muses in a higher level of Elysium, as they were no longer wanted in the intermediary realm between gods and men.

"By the light you exude, I can see that you're a singer of songs. Do you sing of me? I say, do you sing of love?"

Julien said he knew the idea of love, but had never experienced it.

"You loved your mother, did you not?" said Eros. "And you must love music and poetry. What about the forest, twilight, a fireplace? Castles and balls, costumes and finery?"

"I did not think that is what you meant by love," said Julien.

"And might there not be something else your unhappy heart might love? Zoe, perhaps?"

Julien admitted to not yet understanding his bond with the girl, and Eros praised him for the suspension of judgment.

"Know that the path you have taken reveals itself as you walk it," said Eros. "Stop to brood and it will disappear."

"But how can I walk this path if I can barely stand?" asked Julien. "I don't even think this is real. I think I'm in Venice, passed out inside some ridiculous contraption made by set designers from the opera."

"Even if that were true, wouldn't you like to go a little bit further? What about finding the Apple of the Hesperides?"

"I see you know everything, don't you?" replied Julien. "You know what I'm supposed to do. That means you could help me."

"Indeed. Perhaps you should convince me to help you."

"How would I do that?"

"Isn't it obvious?" said Eros with a charming laugh. "Love the task before you. Love the adventure. Love the thought of saving Zoe. Absolute affirmation, absolute trust."

"But where do I begin to find the old gods, even with…" Julien paused. "Even with a magic sea shell and a divine teenager from the beginning of time? Since I've arrived the only path I've found has led me to a necropolis."

"No," Eros corrected, "it led you to me. This is an artist's studio. Have you not heard of the art form whose summit is called the *magnum opus*?"

Julien shook his head.

"Why, it is the *Ars Regia,*" said Eros with haughtiness. "The Royal Art." Suddenly his voice turned strange, as though the very breath of the universe were speaking through him in some coded language. He seemed briefly to glow, engulfed in a flame of light:

"*The tradition by which obscure heroes may win as their 'bride' a mysterious occult force, allowing them to integrate their virility on the spiritual plane so as to become kings in other worlds.*"

Eros returned to his normal state as a handsome youth and bounded out of the studio as Julien hurriedly followed. They wound through the spiral of the necropolis back to the center with its dry fountain, statue of Apollo, and nine skeletal muses, and from there walked out into the afternoon sun, whereupon Julien asked whether the island had a name.

"It is called Aesthetikos and was once a land where the gods and muses worked in communion with artists," explained Eros, "providing inspiration that would descend upon them in visions and dreams. It has become a necropolis because man no longer seeks his artistic inspiration from the divine part of himself. There are no more artist-heroes who conquer the higher realms to create illuminated works. Now you have what's called art-for-art's-sake. Very refined, very late, and very brief. Soon your world will become uglier than you can possibly imagine."

Julien asked why the higher powers did not intervene, but Eros calmly replied that everything in the cosmos had its place in the divine order, and that gods and spirits were under orders not to interfere with mankind's free will. "We can only 'intervene,' as you call it, when man calls upon us."

The duo reached the top of the cliffs overlooking the sea, with the Scorpitaria below, bobbing in the waters while absorbing the sun's rays.

Eros pronounced her a fine ship that would take Julien to his destiny, provided that the measure of his heart proved worthy. "But there is something you must possess before you can ever hope to find the old gods," he warned. "It's neither an idea you think nor a hope in which you believe, but something that is part of you, as sure as you have a right arm and a left, a left leg and a right, and a head atop your shoulders, by which you form a five-pointed star, the symbol of Venus."

"Yes?" replied Julien. "What must I possess?"

"The double-ouroboros."

"I see the single just won't do..." Julien muttered.

Eros told him to go to the island of Bellikos, which was devoted to the god Ares and the place where immortal warriors practiced their swordplay. It was there he would find Achilles. When Julien pleaded for Eros to join him, the youth said that this was not how the Royal Art worked. "You must spend time alone in order for Nature to do the work of transforming you," he explained. "We will reunite at successive stages."

And then just as swiftly as Eros had appeared he was gone, dissolved into the ether like a candle's flame extinguished.

Julien bounded down the boulders, hopped along the stones of the jetty, and leapt on top of the Scorpitaria. Before dropping inside, he removed his velvet coat and threw it into the sea along with his white shirt. He might have felt powerful and free, as when he bared his torso as Count Wrathchild, but Julien was too weary. Inside the vessel he drank from the waterskin before ordering the sea shell to take him to the island of Bellikos.

As the ship headed out to sea Julien lay on the floor gazing out the portholes at the dimming sunlight, seized with a fear of the interminable night. He pulled the animal skins over himself and curled into a ball as the ship descended and monsters of the sea began to swirl about it. His life flashed before him once more, and it felt as though entire parts of him were being melted off by way of an agonizing process, stripping him down to the bone. His torments continued until the energy was spent and he lapsed into torpor.

When he awoke Julien found that the Scorpitaria had berthed and was recharging in the morning light. White foam splashed against the portholes as the ship violently rocked. Struggling to steady himself, Julien rummaged through the supply bin, where he found a black chemise with no sleeves. He threw it on, climbed out, and leapt upon a large rock. Surveying the situation, he saw that he was 50 yards from shore — except there was no shore, only a cliff. He had no choice but to jump in the sea, try to keep from drowning, and let the waves take him in.

With his clothes heavy and hands wet, ascending the cliff's face proved an agonizing test. Halfway up a nauseating fear overtook Julien, followed by the even more horrifying revelation that it would be more treacherous to climb down than continue. He pushed on with such determination that suddenly it seemed Julien Stanwyck did not even exist, and all that remained was the will of a nameless man and the task at hand.

When he finally touched flat earth, Julien saw two sandaled feet standing at the edge of the cliff, followed by a hand. He grabbed it and was pulled to safety, collapsing exhausted on his back. Panting heavily, he looked up to see the golden locks of Achilles backlit by the sun of Apollo in the morning sky.

"You must be the hero Eros told me was coming," the great warrior said, tossing down a wineskin. "Drink this. It's laced with ambrosia, food of the gods. Hermes brings a skin of it whenever the time warrants."

Julien rose and drank greedily. Then he asked whether Achilles too was a god. The warrior explained that he had once been mortal like Julien, but had won conditional immortality and ascended the Great Chain of Being from the underworld to the Elysian realm. Julien had thought that Hades was the underworld and that the world was simply the world, but Achilles countered that in the Age of Iron the two were merging and would soon become indistinguishable.

"I've been sent to ask the old gods for help," said Julien, "for just that reason."

Achilles had no idea where to find them, as the communion between gods and men was like a broken sword that had to be mended. He and the myrmidons occupied the middle sector of the broken blade, and had lost touch with beings both below and above it. Julien explained that he had just come from Aesthetikos and that it was now a necropolis.

"Then Olympus is truly fallen," said Achilles. "Our race may very well go extinct."

He proceeded to tell the story of how he had once summoned the Fates to show him what was unfolding, and how they had revealed a world of slaves made equal to their masters, barbarians aided by the state, and tyrants voted in by the populace. "Would you fight for these people of the future?" Achilles queried contemptuously. "And yet the inscription at the Temple of Delphi was 'Know Thyself.' I would not fight for these men of the underworld, who deserve to lose their homelands for forgetting us, their kindred spirits. But everything in the cosmos serves the level above it, and so I and the myrmidons would still fight for fighting's sake, for such is the disposition Nature has given us."

"Then our struggle is not for the people?" asked Julien.

"Not for the rabble, the plebs, the masses. Even in the Age of Gold they did not know of Mount Olympus. If they are of the servant caste they think only of bestial needs, and of material comfort if they are merchants. We fight for Zeus, Hermes, Aphrodite—and for the one who created even them. For they too look up in wonder, just as mortals do, according to the law of correspondence."

Julien praised the man for his wisdom, remarking that such was not usually the purview of warriors.

"Eternity does that to you," said Achilles.

The men had reached a camp made of well appointed tents, where Achilles and the myrmidons lived separately from the island's other warrior heroes. Julien ate olives, barley bread, and cheese before falling fast asleep. The following day they walked through shrublands to a forest of pine trees, where the light from Apollo was sparse. Handing Julien a wooden training sword and shield, Achilles told him that he had much to learn if he was going to win the favors of a goddess.

"I was told to awaken the old gods," said Julien.

And that included the goddesses, said Achilles. Did he not arrive via the feminine elements of water and earth? Julien would not find Olympus even with the help of Pegasus, Achilles explained, for it could not be found in the elements of fire and air. "Your sea shell—symbol of Aphrodite—will take you where you need to go, provided you pass each stage of your trials and acquire the double-serpent."

"What is this double-serpent?" asked Julien. "Do you possess it?"

"Of course I do," replied Achilles. "I would hardly have reached Elysium otherwise. But I earned mine through war in the Age of Gold and you live in the Age of Iron. The path I took is closed to you. You're right-handed, correct?"

Julien affirmed that he was, and Achilles instructed him to place the shield in his right and the sword in his left. Julien protested, saying that he preferred to wield a sword with his strong arm. But it was precisely for this reason, Achilles told him, that he should do the opposite. Julien voiced his doubts as to the prospect of defeating the world's greatest warrior armed in such a way.

"You're not supposed to *defeat* me," Achilles roared with laughter. "I'm training you. You get stronger just by looking at me. And when I look at you, by the way, I see what looks like a skeleton sprouted from a Hydra's tooth."

Julien dropped his guard, saying he was at his weakest point and was merely a singer of songs.

"That may be your vocation," said Achilles with an exaggerated swing at Julien's head, causing him to duck, "but that's not what you *are*. You're a hero, otherwise you wouldn't be here."

As the days passed Julien grew stronger. But his old rage continued to assert itself, exposing weaknesses to the mighty Achilles. Nevertheless the great warrior managed to temper the Martian energies of Julien's horoscope, which lordship had never properly harnessed. And when the light of Apollo had tanned Julien's pallor and his muscles began to flourish, Achilles lent him his bronze sword, which Julien used to cut the legs of his leather breeches, turning them into "peplum-shorts" that freed his thickened legs for better movement.

Then one day, while training on a grassy hill spotted with orchids, Achilles asked Julien whether he feared death. Julien replied that he was unsure whether it qualified as fear, but that he had been obsessed with it all his life. Then he turned the question back onto the great warrior, with respect to the time when he had been a mortal.

"Death never once entered my mind," replied Achilles. "I focused on just one thing: the fall of my enemy. And fall he always did — until an arrow found my heel, the weak spot written in my fate."

Julien wondered whether, upon reflection, Achilles did not feel he had been reckless, given the fact that no battle held a guarantee of victory.

"You still do not understand how the cosmos works, my mortal friend," said Achilles. "It's precisely because the outcome was uncertain that I ensured my victory, willing it more strongly than my opponent. Many were bigger, stronger, and better trained, but I had unraveled the Mystery of Nike and therefore victory was always mine. Never doubt the wisdom of the gods: cowardice attracts blades like a magnet, while courage makes entire armies retreat. But there's one more secret to the mystery of the goddess of victory: you must be unafraid of death. It is a paradox, for only by acting from a perspective already beyond death does one escape it."

Julien asked whether, in the realm he currently inhabited, he was already beyond death, but Achilles explained that he was only here provisionally. He had not yet earned his immortality, but the gods had granted temporary access to the Olympian dimension.

"Then they're awake?" asked Julien.

"Of course they're awake," replied Achilles. "How could gods not be awake when they live in eternity?"

"Then they must be expecting me," Julien said morosely. "After all, they have called me here."

Achilles affirmed the notion.

"Then why don't they? — "

"Stop asking why!" Achilles blurted out. "This is way above you! For all you know there are a thousand others going through the same thing. And from what the Fates have shown me, that's not nearly enough. But I suggest you start acting like the only one who can save your world from the destruction that merchants and servants can wreak."

When Achilles deemed Julien ready for his final trial, he summoned the myrmidons and the men formed squads for battle. The great warrior's loyal followers used their weapons merely to sting Julien, as a full blow would disintegrate his astral body and send him tumbling back to the underworld. But as they could not be killed Julien was allowed to fight with a real sword and deal lethal blows. When the melee was done—a blinding blur that took Julien completely beyond himself—several myrmidons said they would have been slain in the mortal realm and congratulated Julien for his prowess. The fracas finished, Julien gazed across the terrain to find Eros standing at the cliffs overlooking the sea.

Achilles acknowledged Eros with a bow of his head then turned to Julien, saying that his time on Bellikos was done. He presented several items to aid him on his mission: a pair of tall black leather sandals suitable for a hero, and two black leather cuffs. The right was inlaid with a golden ouroboros, while the left one featured the same figure in silver. He also told Julien to keep the bronze sword he held in his hand, and with a sideways cock of his head, a knowing smile, and a gentle aspiration, bid the apprentice on his way.

Julien walked proudly across the field to join Eros, and together they gazed down the cliff at the Scorpitaria glistening below. Julien felt a strange fondness for the magical contraption, in which he had glimpsed all the monsters of the abyss. Once again he asked whether the handsome youth would like to accompany him in the submersible ship, but Eros said he would meet Julien on the next island, and promptly dissolved into the ether.

Julien shrugged his shoulders, placed the sandals and cuffs in his knapsack, and turned his attention to the problem of reaching the ship. With no means of descent, he raised his sword in a salute to the sun-god Apollo and leapt. After the grotesque but all-too-familiar feeling of freefall and splashdown, Julien paddled to the Scorpitaria, tossed up the sword and sack, and climbed on top. After laying out his things to dry, he practiced his swordplay in the sun, as pure and naked as the statue of a Hellenic hero.

How long had he been with Achilles? In this dimension time held no meaning; there was only action and transformation. Julien felt incredible, beyond anything he had ever known. The muscles of his chest and arms had filled out, and his legs had become sculpted as well. "It's fun to play gods and heroes," he laughed to himself.

His exercises were abruptly halted, however, by the realization that Eros had not revealed his next destination. Julien's old instincts returned as he suddenly feared being stuck in limbo for all eternity, and the fear was founded when the hatch would not open and the ship began to hum.

Julien watched with wide-eyed horror for the Scorpitaria to submerge, but it remained on the surface. He consoled himself with the idea that the next island must be so close there had been no need for Eros to mention it. He also thought perhaps the sea shell already knew the destination. Slowly adjusting to the top of the ship as it cruised, Julien saw the tails of what he surmised were mermaids splashing in the water, and took pleasure in the thought that they guarded the great island of Bellikos, home of the heroes.

In a symbolic gesture of the affirmation Eros had required of him, Julien threw his boots into the sea and strapped on the sandals that Achilles had given him, along with the cuff bracelets: gold on the right, silver on the left. Then he lay back and rested in the sun from his long trials, watching as the sun sank into the sea with a miasmic swirl of purples, pinks, and oranges.

He was awakened in the darkness of night by a splash of cold water. Julien roused to orient himself, but what he saw in the moonlight filled him with apprehension, for he soon ascertained that he had not gone out to sea, but was drifting in a circle about the island of Bellikos. He was indeed in a kind of limbo, at the mercy of the phantasmagoric vessel whose hatch still would not open. Chill water washed over him once again, after which he could see a dozen female heads peering above the water's surface.

Surely these sea-maidens can help me, Julien thought.

But as he prepared to address them, they filled the silent night with shrill laughter. Swirling around the Scorpitaria mockingly, they used their tails to drench him before resuming their whine and wail. Julien confirmed that these were perfidious sirens — not protectors of the island of heroes, but its antagonists. When they leapt from the water the moonlight revealed them in all their grotesqueness: their obese torsos were covered in blue-green seaweed motifs like tattoos, barnacles were stuck to the nipples of their soggy breasts, and fish hooks were rammed in their noses like jewelry.

Julien waited as patiently as a proverbial fisherman while the sirens continued their mockery. With cunning and guile — and sword concealed behind his back — he bowed his head to signal surrender, then dangled his legs over the side of the ship as an invitation for the sirens to pull him into the depths. When one of them swam close and prepared to grab his legs, Julien snatched the creature by the hair, withdrew his sword from behind, and beheaded it with one stroke.

With the head in one hand Julien turned the lever on the hatch and found that it now opened. He cast the still-cackling head into the sea, threw his sack and sword into the ship and dropped inside, marching past the painting of Perseus to the navigation shell.

"I've beheaded the monster!" Julien shouted. "Now take me to the next destination!"

But nothing changed as the minutes passed, and the Scorpitaria neither altered its course nor submerged. Julien lay on the floor with his teeth clenched in frustration, wiping the siren's blood from his sword. As he ruminated fruitlessly over what to do, something caught his eye. Peeking out from the waist of his peplum-shorts was a strange line which wavered between light and darkness. The skin of his belly was bronze from the sun of Bellikos, while that which lay below the garment was as pale as a Gothic moon.

The contrast evoked an image from his time in Pygmalion's studio on the island of Aesthetikos. Just before Eros had appeared, Julien had watched every form of feminine beauty coalesce before his eyes. At the final moment he had caught a glimpse of some impossible ideal of exquisite perfection. Not a "dream girl," as they were called in the parlor songs of the day, but the energy of a living goddess — a dark and lonely goddess.

Julien's thought-stream next showed him all he held dear, everything he considered noble and beautiful. On the one hand were stories of ancient glories, the legacy of his race at its loftiest, the castle that for a moment had been his. And then he saw that within this culture won by swords were shimmering pianos, from which men such as himself created art that raised the soul. Finally he saw all the delicious confections of late-stage decadent civilization, with its cafes and salons and ladies wrapped in silk and satin.

Julien shook his head as though awakening from a reverie and set down the sword. He had trained with Achilles, but Achilles he was not. He had acquired combat skills, but he was much more than a warrior. He walked calmly to the bow of the vessel and removed the magic seashell from its pedestal. Lifting it to his ear, he thought he could hear a melancholy waltz in an empty ballroom — empty save for some mysterious figure awaiting his arrival. He whispered into the shell as if into a lover's ear, asking to be taken to Eros, and a moment later the Scorpitaria descended into the Aegean.

CHAPTER EIGHT

AFTER TIME in the depths of Neptune, in which the newfound warrior side of Julien battled with the artist in him, which counter-attacked with strange magic that made him writhe on the floor of the vessel in agony, the Scorpitaria finally pulled into a tranquil cove with clear waters and a beach of white sand.

Reveling in the novel sensation of walking on the beach, Julien was greeted by bright sunlight and a balmy breeze. No ascent up a treacherous cliff would be required of him this time, as he was greeted by a large staircase flanked by two grand urns. Julien bounded up the steps eagerly and was relieved to find neither the desolation of the necropolis nor the fields and forests of Bellikos. Instead there were sculpted pathways marked by herm statues, pomegranate trees, heliotrope flowers, and streams cascading down the mountains in the distance.

One moment Julien was alone and the next Eros was standing beside him in white peplum and golden sandals, his torso bared. He had come to welcome Julien to the island of Erotikos, where he lived with his retinue of Erotes: Anteros, Himeros, Pothos, Hedylogos, Hymenaios, and Hermaphroditus.

"Many consider this the most beautiful island in Elysium," Eros said, "for it is devoted to the force that binds together everything else in the cosmos." Inspecting the leather cuffs which Achilles had given Julien, he nodded approvingly at the golden ouroboros on the right and silver on the left. "Very good. Now, before your trials begin…"

Julien protested, asking what trials there could possibly be in paradise.

"But has not love its own tests and trials?" replied Eros rhetorically. "First you'll first need to drink this philter—why do you float that expression?"

"Because the last time I was given a potion," said Julien, "I was locked inside something resembling Jules Verne's entry into the Science & Industry wing of the World's Fair. And before that I watched a castle full of people drink absinthe and chew each other's ears off."

"That was the wormwood," said Eros matter-of-factly. "Regina's absinthe is distilled with a wormwood that 'worms' its way into the human brain, where it receives occult vibrations according to her commands. You might call it a 'mind-virus.'"

"Regina, you say?" said Julien, dumbfounded. "As in Regina Grossman?"

"Loyal servant of the embodied principle of inversion known as Satan," replied Eros. "In a few years she will be elected Prime Minister, after which she will declare herself Empress of Gaul."

Eros explained that mortal women were ruled by the Supreme Author's left hand. Although religious cults demonized them as evil, they were in fact neutral. "When man is good, honors the gods, and instills divine order," he said, "then woman assists man as the moon reflects the sun. When he becomes weak, she enacts her function of pulling everything down to the feminine elements of water and earth, to the womb of chaos and matriarchal collectivism. Then man must reconnect with his center, find the bridge to the closed palace of the king within his heart, and begin a new cycle of civilization, at which point woman again becomes his loyal helpmeet.

"Until then," Eros continued, "she will fulfill her Satanic function of negating everything man has built but has failed to adequately defend, and will usher in a reign of ugliness, stupidity, and falsehood. The 20th century has already dawned, and you, my dear Julien, have come much later in the course of humanity than you know. As the earth's poles begin their magnetic reversal, women will marshal in the new cosmic order. They will become the politicians, professors, and administrators of justice. Children will rule their parents, wives their husbands. Art, literature, and all creative endeavors will be done by subverters, and then by computational machines. Individual minds will be brought under centralization, controlled by electronic devices. Finally, the most savage tribes of mankind will enslave the natives of Europa, and women will administer the entire process, calling it progress. And the populace will be so hypnotized by material comfort and poisonous frivolity that it will barely notice what is happening."

The rage of Achilles roared inside of Julien.

"There is more, if you can bear it," continued Eros. "In the world that is dawning, woman will discover two superpowers that will hasten the collapse of civilization. The first is whoredom, which means absolute receptivity, making no distinction between the qualitative differences of men, which is what absolute means. As everything in the cosmos comes with its opposite according to the law of polarity, the other side of whoredorm's coin will cause woman to adopt impossible standards in the selection of a husband. Next she will discover absolute compassion, which will permit her to defend every form of savagery. Even as the knife is twisting inside her, woman will say to her barbarian killer, 'I forgive you,' because she has discovered that this auto-genocidal compassion is the greatest weapon with which to punish her men for becoming weak. And the converse of absolute compassion will be draconian despotism towards anything that stands in its way as the rule of law."

Julien shook his head, saying that he had been obsessed with women all his life and yet had never fallen in love. Eros pointed out that it was perhaps not woman he sought, but the possibilities provided by possession of the double-serpent.

Julien demanded to know what it was.

"Drink the philter and find out."

"What will it do?" asked Julien, examining the bottle in the sunlight.

Eros explained that the potion would cause a temporary change in the polarity of his being, causing him to re-center his astral body around lunar and Venusian energies. He would still be himself, but he would appear to others in this realm as a woman. Julien could not understand why, after all he had just been told, he was now being told to become female. Eros explained that it was merely a stage in the magistery of the Royal Art, and that it might bring delicate *frissons*, in addition to knowledge of the Supreme Author's left hand.

"You're not going to drop me into a pack of amazons, are you?" Julien asked, removing the bottle's stopper.

"No," replied Eros. "We're going to the Grotto of Lesbos."

Julien paused, then downed the potion in a single gulp.

As the liquid took effect Julien felt a pleasantness slowly infiltrate his sense-perceptions, as though he had stepped into a warm bath. His struggles and sorrows, his compulsive urge to understand his quest instead of allowing it to unfold, of trying to dominate everything he encountered, all the rage Achilles had extracted from him and tempered as a polished blade—all of that dissolved into a free and fluidic state he had never known. Everything came alive in ways he had never experienced, and he perceived reality not as something to be conquered, but as something to be savored and beheld with wonder.

As they strolled across the island, Eros instructed Julien in the doctrine of cinnabar. The ore was seldom used on earth, he explained, but guardians of the Hyperborean tradition had discovered something peculiar about it. "Cinnabar is largely toxic to mortals," said Eros, "but the ancients discovered that it could be melted down and the steam collected, which could be re-heated with quicksilver, otherwise known as Mercury, whose power of neutrality is symbolized by the staff of Hermes. When this distilled substance was cooled, it left a polished crystal with the red tint of cinnabar but without the toxicity. This led the sages to infer that there must be a spirit trapped in everything designed by the Supreme Author, a kind of cosmic programming, and that anything can be purified of its grosser material elements to shine as it did in the mind of its creator — including you."

The pair reached a grotto where voices could be heard behind bushes of bougainvillea. Julien asked what Eros wished him to do, to which the youth replied that he should begin by observing, then move on to experiences, as initiation was based on knowledge gained from experience in the numinal dimension. Once he felt sated, Julien was to call upon Eros in order to be taken to the next destination.

Julien parted the bougainvillea and entered the steaming grotto, where what he found was beyond any artist's imagining of ancient sapphic voluptuousness. There was a pool surrounded by dozens of women in various states of undress — spanning from flowing Grecian robes to complete nudity — in poses of supreme languor. In groups of twos and threes they bathed, rubbed oil on each other's bodies, and sat with their arms wrapped around each other drinking wine, whispering, and indolently waving fans. There was a constant chorus of partial, stolen, and passing caresses: tender touches and soft kisses, reassuring embraces, sliding hands and batting eyes, all of this enacted with the subtlety of flapping butterfly wings.

Julien watched in fascination from the edge of the grotto until two fetching damsels in white robes approached him with welcoming gestures. This led Julien to conclude that the philter had worked and that the women took him to be one of their own, a soul of Lesbos freshly arrived. With complete nonchalance, as though Julien were hardly even there, they escorted him around the pool to a canopy draped with fabric, the grass covered with carpets and cushions. In dulcet tones that were strange and yet which Julien seemed to understand, they spoke softly while pampering him in a relaxed manner, brushing his long curls, weaving flowers into his hair, and rubbing his body with scented oils.

Slowly their pettings grew from faintly suggestive to flagrantly erotic, causing Julien to stir, as what they were doing could no longer be ignored. Before he could speak they lay him on his back, and their hands and lips began to explore his body. Julien had known a number of *menages à trois* in his time as the libertine Count Wrathchild, but this was a new world.

There was no ego seeking to dominate the women, for he had become one of them. The pleasure he experienced had no precise location, nor did it have a particular goal. He was neither trying to force a climax nor hold one back, and so wave after wave of ecstasy swept over him, and his own hands and lips sought the bodies of his partners. Together they became one symphonic tapestry of voluptuousness, like the music of Wagner's *Tristan,* ever in motion but never reaching a final resolution. Each ecstatic rise merely returned to a resting state of arousal before rising yet again. Julien was so deliciously delirious he thought it would never end, and he stayed with the women of Lesbos until all sense of time was lost.

But then one afternoon a series of images assailed his reveries. First the simple poles supporting the canopy above him became Doric columns. Then his tent transformed into a temple. The temple coagulated in Julien's imagination until it rose into a grand edifice in the Beaux Arts style, replicating itself horizontally into a stately city. Then the female flesh in which Julien had been immersed for so long suddenly appeared in states of *deshabille.* Julien beheld not legs smooth from olive oil but shimmering silk stockings, and not Hellenic robes but tight corsets. He shook his head back and forth, wincing, as exquisite perfumes overcame him in an olfactory hallucination, followed by the scent of cognac, cigars, and the warm pastille-scented breath of a panting little *grisette* begging for virile caresses back at his studio in Paris.

Julien leapt up from the vision and exited the grotto as fast as he could, calling out to Eros inside his mind. When he reached the island's main thoroughfare, he found the handsome youth with an expectant smile on his face, asking how he felt.

"Like I want my cock back," Julien deadpanned.

Prodded by Eros, he confessed that his experience had been rapturous, fascinating, intoxicating, illuminating, and, in the end, simply different. Eros said that the wisdom he had gained was evident on his cuffs, which Julien inspected. After his time with Achilles, the golden serpent on the right glowed, while the silver one on the left was dull. Now the right side was dull and the left illumined. Julien asked what it meant.

"That you are progressing," replied Eros. "And you look radiant, by the way."

He explained that the trials on Bellikos had hardened Julien, while his time in the Grotto of Lesbos had softened him. And now his journey would continue at the Garden of the Hermaphrodites. When Julien asked whether he was still in feminine form, Eros explained that the philter was slowly wearing off, and that he would appear precisely as he was meant to.

Soon they reached a fastidiously tended garden of hyacinth on the banks of a narrow river, with another elaborate garden, this one of dianthus, on the other side. In the center of the river a statue of Hermaphroditus rose from the waters, which were neither hot nor cool, but tepid.

The souls who made pilgrimage here did not gather in twos and threes, nor did they lounge in groups as they had in the Lesbos colony. They were self-sufficient and self-involved, and while they enjoyed being among their kind they did not often interact. Most of their time was spent in gymnastic gyrations, rituals done under the sun by day and under the moon by night. The hermaphrodites stretched and pulled, then crouched and crunched in contractions of ecstatic release. When they sought the company of another, they swam the river to one side when they felt active and the other when they felt receptive. But the polarity of the two riverbank gardens was different for each soul, so that the flowers of hyacinth and the flowers of dianthus were always populated by an ever-changing yet equal balance of active and passive energies.

As time passed Julien could not avoid their advances, which had all the voluptuousness of the women in whose company he had just been. The writhing movements of their bodies were often identical to the sapphic souls, except that there was a force behind the hermaphroditic caresses, albeit in a strange kind of inverted expression. It was as though they were performing not the action itself but the shadow of it, which contained a great mystery. Often the raptures would suddenly rise only for the lover to suddenly pull away and simply lie beside Julien, with both of them in a state of suspended arousal, gazing up at the stars.

If the volcanic pool of Lesbos had threatened to hold Julien in its sultry moistness forever, the tepid stream with the two riverbanks was even more powerful. The longer he stayed in the Garden of the Hermaphrodites, the more his tormented passages through the realm of Neptune would vanish from his mind. And yet the absence of struggle would leave Julien feeling directionless, without the motivation and purpose of his divine mission.

And then one exquisite evening at twilight, while squirming to remold his form, Julien's consciousness finally reached full understanding of the two snakelike energies that ran from his generative region up through his spine, his heart, and his mind, where they reached their highest vibration. He looked immediately at his leather cuffs and found that they had both been neutralized, for neither the gold nor the silver glowed, but rested equally in their passive state. Julien hastily exited the gardens and made his way to the central pathway of

Erotikos, where Eros stood with the radiant evening star of Hesperus over his shoulder.

"If you could see yourself now in the pool of Narcissus," said the eternal youth, "you would truly fall in love with your own reflection, for Achilles has made you strong, Lesbos has made you soft, and the Garden of Hermaphrodites has made you a panther."

Julien said that his looks had always been an embarrassment to him, no more than a means of satiating his carnal lust. When Eros asked what lust he might be feeling now, Julien replied that he felt none, and asked whether he had been cured of something.

"Perhaps," Eros replied.

They had come to the next part of the island, where waterfalls plummeted down the mountains and gathered in a pool surrounded by stone pedestals, upon which stood male figures of perfect Hellenic beauty, as if they had been sculpted by the great Phidias himself. After assuming statuesque postures on the pedestals, the figures would plunge into the bracing pool, which cooled their generative region so that, when they climbed back into the light of Apollo, no single part of their anatomy drew attention away from the harmony of their form. Then one by one they would walk to a nearby area of soft dirt to grapple, as each pressed his strength against the other, feeling his own in the process.

"Behold the Basin of Adonis," said Eros. "Where souls gifted with male beauty come to replenish themselves among their kindred. Here you will finally cease to resent your beauty and see it as a gift of the gods."

Julien said that these souls were like the gods, so great was their aura of power and magnificence.

"In a certain sense you are correct," explained Eros. "These souls were once mortals who underwent the deification process, modeling themselves on immortal gods and heroes in order to become like them. As for strength, you have not even begun to discover it, for there are three stages behind you, and the philter, in case you haven't noticed, has completely worn off."

Julien looked down at his hands and splayed his fingers, those ten digits which had pressed piano keys and caressed lovers, wielded a sword and fought with warriors. He shook out his limbs, tilted his head from side to side, raised his shoulders and then dropped them back into place, and flexed the muscles of his chest and back. An energy pulsed within him of terrifying potential, and Eros suggested he immediately plunge into the basin. Julien, silent and awestruck, threw down his rucksack, removed his sandals and peplum-shorts, keeping only the leather cuffs on his body, and dove into the pool.

When he emerged and stood upon a pedestal among the others, he felt stripped and purified in a state of absolute nakedness. Later, in a dimension beyond time, he was greeted by the kindred spirits. They would begin by wrapping their clutches around the base of each other's skull, bracing their forearms against their opponent's chest. Then they would begin a chess game of shifting dynamics. There was no right or left in Julien's body now, just one flowing power emanating from his solar plexus.

When he had sufficiently swam, grappled, and posed like the gods, Julien became filled with memories of Zoe and Zapfe and the evil overtaking Europa, and knew it was time to continue his mission. He dressed, nodded to each fellow Adonis, and joined Eros, who sat on a stone admiring the beautiful physiques.

The cold water and hot sun made Julien's body feel taut and sculpted. None of his vital energies wandered from his center. Whenever he flexed his right arm, invoking his time with Achilles, his left arm would immediately counter by arching its wrist and delicately stroke the area of his heart, recollecting his time in the Grotto of Lesbos. With these two energies simultaneously activated, Julien's consciousness recalibrated, sinking down into the self-sufficient state he had experienced in the Garden of Hermaphrodites, with the front of his generative region active and the back passive. But now this neutered state was instantly pulled upward towards the gods, into the pedestal poses of the Basin of Adonis. Julien perceived the image of a quaternary, with Achilles to the right, Lesbos to the left, Hermaphroditus below, and Adonis above. It was a kind of cross inside a circle, like the wheels on the chariot Achilles kept outside his tent. And somehow he — the new Julien — was at the center of the cross in the middle of the circle.

Eros led him to a nearby pond so he could behold the changes he felt, and what he saw was greater than he could ever have imagined. The hard angles of Julien's jaw had been attenuated, and his sardonic lips were now as plush as those of a damsel in a Pre-Raphaelite painting. Instead of betraying a troubled soul, his eyes told of an enlightened spirit, while his chestnut hair had lost the agitation of its curls, and cascaded past his shoulders in waves golden from the sun. The changes to his physique were even more astonishing, as the morbid pallor of his complexion had turned to bronze, and his skeletal physique was now the Platonic ideal of a Hellenic hero. His broad shoulders had been properly filled out, supported by muscles, hitherto unknown, around the base of his neck, back, and chest. His slender abdomen now revealed musculature previously hidden, and his legs were thickly sculpted from ankle to thigh.

Gazing at him in admiration, Eros congratulated Julien on acquiring the double-ouroboros, and Julien glanced down at the cuffs bequeathed by Achilles. Each one featured two serpents knotted together, so that the head of the golden snake bit the tail of the silver one, and vice versa. Still, Julien wondered how he could possess something he still did not understand.

"You had a gift for poetry and music before you knew it, did you not?" said Eros. "Each creative act in the cosmos is the result of a masculine, generative principle, and a feminine, productive one. But now the active jaws of the golden serpent are attached to the passive end of the feminine serpent, while the actively feminine mouth is attached to the passive masculine tail."

“In one continuous circuit,” said Julien.

“Precisely, which means that a single power, the *prima materia*, animates the entire cosmos, generative as well as productive. This divine spark now courses through your nervous system, giving you a much stronger presence within the Astral Light.”

Eros suggested testing it by finding Zoe’s vibration in the Astral Light and projecting an image of Julien’s transformed self towards it. The ether would carry the information, coded as divine intelligence, and her consciousness would perceive it.

Julien gazed at his reflection in the pond and closed his eyes, invoking Zoe while still holding the image of himself in his mind’s eye. When he felt like an archer locked onto his target, he expended the image as if improvising at the piano. A moment later his consciousness received a return image from Zoe, showing her own transformation from a charming tomboy into a true Ganymede, her soul’s noble image of itself.

“Zoe, too, has been on the path of cinnabar,” said Eros. “And now it is time for you to plead your case to the old gods. I’m quite sure, Julien, you now know which one you are destined to find.”

Julien felt the trial of a new riddle, and knew he would not solve it with logic and reason. He closed his eyes, drew his fingernails across his heart, and spoke the name “Aphrodite.”

“Indeed,” confirmed Eros. “But you will not find her here, for she waits in the land of Aegyptus.”

“Why is she not in Hellas with the other Olympians?” Julien queried.

Eros explained that the embodied form of Aphrodite accessible to Julien passed through his horoscope, the map of his soul’s dynamic energies. The planet Venus was in its detriment in the sign of Scorpio, and so Julien’s personal Aphrodite lay hiding in the original land of the Mysteries, in a cave near Luxor, where she awaited a hero acting in the name of a higher cause. “She seeks to be loved, not feared. Needed, not shunned,” Eros explained. “But her erotic allure is more volatile than any other form of Aphrodite, so be warned. Desire destroys the bond between gods and heroes. You will have to know, in every cell of your being, that you are worthy of her, and not merely fascinated."

In the flick of an eye the handsome youth was gone, and Julien commenced retracing his steps across the island of Erotikos, recalling his experiences as he had passed through the Mysteries of Sex. When he reached the beach, he found the Scorpitaria's circuitry pulsing brightly with Apollonian light. He climbed inside with a feeling of triumph, which was key to the Royal Art. Julien had seen the light of the Olympian realm but it had not overwhelmed him, absorbing him into itself and erasing his identity. He had endured a seven-stage ego death, become a warrior, a "woman," a divine androgyne, and the very model of a Greek god. And yet through it all he had maintained his sense of "I, Julien Stanwyck," even as the man he believed himself to be was constantly destroyed and reborn.

After speaking his destination into the seashell Julien lay down on the animal skins, his head propped on a cushion. As the ship pulled out to sea his gaze fell first upon the heroic frescoes painted on the walls, then shifted to the portholes, through which he watched the Scorpitaria descend into Poseidon's realm. Julien had no fear of sea monsters or inner torments now, and soon fell into a deep sleep so that his transformation could solidify. By the time he awoke he had already reached the Land of the Pharaohs.

He drank water heartily, noting that it felt more powerful inside his new physique than the finest cognac ever had. From the supply bin he withdrew a fresh sleeveless chemise of midnight navy, and found two items that had not been there before: a belt and sheath for his sword, and a regal cloak made not of ancient wool or linen, but plush black velvet. He fastened it with a golden shoulder clasp depicting a Sagittarian archer with the tail of a scorpion, climbed out through the hatch, and leapt into the shallow waters of the Nile delta filled with anticipation.

Eros stood waiting among a grove of palm trees wearing his familiar smile. Julien now thought of the divine youth as a friend, thinking to himself that man could indeed forge bonds with the old gods, working together for the land of Europa.

"I've arranged a new mode of transportation for you," said Eros, "that will help expand your consciousness beyond the confines of space and time. You must begin to see reality as a threefold structure comprising your physical life back on earth, the inner world of your poetic soul, and the overworld where you are now. These three dimensions of body, soul and spirit are linked not by the course of human events men call 'history,' but higher consanguinities, sympathies, and creative expressions. This chariot is true to the spirit you bear within you, that Hyperborean wellspring containing both the Gothic and the Olympian."

Eros gestured to a nearby grove of acacia shrubs where a metallic monster peeked between the brush. Julien withdrew his sword and cut his way through the thorny bushes, revealing an industrial machine even more fantastic than the Scorpitaria.

"Surely you saw a horseless carriage on the streets of New York?" said Eros.

"Those absurd contraptions spouting steam and making noise?" said Julien as he stared at the vehicle, which looked like the result of a spell cast by the legendary Count Dracula.

"With the advance of man's diabolical technics, this has been the result," explained Eros. "Men of the future call this a motorcar, and this model is called the 'Diablo' and hails from the land of Italia. I have coalesced it out of the ether and modified it to run on the power of Apollo, just like your ship. Not only will it get you to Luxor, which is 400 miles away, but it shows that in spite of the darkness overtaking Europa, man's Gothic imagination lives in eternity. Whenever he wishes, European man can pull fresh possibilities down from the Olympian realm in order to manifest new creations in the terrestrial sphere."

Like a Medieval sigil, the front of the motorcar was emblazoned with a shield depicting a charging bull. "This machine must have been manifested when the Sun was in Taurus," speculated Julien. "And since Taurus is ruled by Aphrodite, it is a beautiful beast that will surely lead me to her."

"Spoken like a true initiate into the Mysteries," said Eros. "Now, let me show you how it works."

CHAPTER NINE

"KNOW THYSELF," Achilles had admonished.

Julien knew himself now — more than ever before. He knew that he thrived on dark, elemental powers. His experience in the sun of Hellas had allowed him to realize himself actively instead of suffering passively from the energies stirring within him. Now he understood the occult doctrine according to which shadow was the product of light.

The mechanical beast was exhilarating. Julien was traveling so fast that the motorcar had actually grown quiet, emitting no more than a dull rumble as he outpaced the noise of the shining phallic-angled pipes in the back. Eros had promised a smooth path of rock-hard earth down the west side of the Nile, and, with the Diablo's power at his fingertips, his body saddled in the smell of its plush leather upholstery, the darkness and desolation that surrounding him — it was the most incredible dream Julien could have ever imagined.

His journey now came to him in images of unparalleled power. It began with the heart-wrenching death of his mother, the fateful meeting with Zoe and the tragic ocean-liner voyage, his sumptuous studio and infamy at Chat Noir, his collaboration with Maurice, and the mystery of his father and the castle. But all this unfolded against a backdrop of civilizational collapse, to which belonged the diabolical Regina Grossman, the assassination of the king, Julien's fugitive flight across Europa, and the meeting with Zapfe on the haunted island of Venice, which placed him in strange machines and shot him beyond everyday reality into the numinal dimension.

When the Great Pyramid passed by in a moonlit blur, Julien pulled his eyes from the roadway and scanned the motorcar's array of knobs and buttons. Eros had told him of a magical means by which he could pass the time on his journey. When he reached the Sphinx, the handsome youth had said, Julien was to activate a special switch and prepare for a surprise. Julien found the right one, and what ensued only made his dreamlike experience all the more incredible.

Music filled the motorcar—familiar music he had heard in Paris—as if an orchestra of gremlins were inside the machine somewhere. The notion caused Julien to laugh at his flight of fancy, as though he had just drunk a glass of poisoned absinthe. But this form of magic came from the technics of the future and the capturing of sound, and what came next was even more astonishing. A human voice filled the speeding Diablo:

> *You're listening to "Dreamers of Decadence" on WNYC, New York. I'm your host, Dee Klein, and that was Gabriel Fauré's beautiful "Pelleas and Melisande" suite. Next I have a great surprise: one of New York's most legendary characters, who left the city at the height of the Decadent era and never returned. Was he a true initiate or a diabolic fraudster? He was never heard from again, but we have a recording of an original wax cylinder made in 1899. So without further pause, allow me to present, live from Chat Noir in Paris, Count Wrathchild and the Castle Ruins:*

And there it was: Maurice on piano, Charles and Pierre on violin and cello, and Julien's voice singing lines he remembered well:

Dark lady in leather, in dreams you conspire
To fill my nights with a longing for bliss

Exciting a thirst that turns burning desire
For a taste of wine from your lips in a kiss

On the winds of a summer my spirit was caught
Though young and naive, in time you would tame
My anger and fear with the wisdom you taught
And return to the world a man not the same

On a bed of black silk you extracted my heart
Then tempered it into a celestial blade
Working the wonders of your secretive art
The angel of night for whom I had prayed

In you I found a path to the sacred and divine
That made me a hero reborn in your shrine

Julien had felt alone his entire life. Only his mother had provided him with the feeling of unconditional love by which he could develop as an artist. Now her place had been taken by an otherworldly presence, and for once Julien felt that he was a character in the mind of the Supreme Author, who had written a story for him which he could never have conceived himself. Words came to him through the Astral Light, attached to the name Meister Eckhart: "The eye through which I see God, and God sees me, are one and the same." Tender tears streamed down Julien's face as he understood that he was alive inside his creator, who was alive inside of him. Like the symbol of the double-serpent, Julien had been chasing God, who had been chasing him, in one continuous circuit of divine energy capable of uniting spirit and matter. "Dead, drugged, or dreaming," said Julien, wiping his cheek, "it makes no difference: what's happening is real."

Eros had also instructed Julien to periodically peer at a dial on the motorcar that kept track of distance. When it reached 400, a bridge across the Nile appeared leading to the city of Luxor, followed by two massive statues called the Colossi of Memnon. He was to commence his search nearby in the Valley of the Queens. When a mass of marl and shale appeared on his right, desolate yet vibrating with energy,

Julien brought the motorcar to a halt, activated the vertical door, and climbed out into the Aegyptian night.

He stretched, drank water from his knapsack, cinched his sword-belt, and wrapped himself in his cloak. Julien followed a path wedged between two cliffs of limestone, which opened out into a silent canyon with rock walls carved into mausoleum entrances. When the far canyon wall came into view, marking the end of the Valley of the Queens, a powerful vibration rattled Julien's gut—and loins. He stood in front of a cave entrance with a wooden door and a large keyhole in the shape of an ankh. Above the entrance was carved a scorpion, which began to glow at Julien's presence. Then a viscous light oozed from its tail, spiraled to the ground, and coalesced. The pool of light caused Julien to leap backwards, and a moment later he faced a scorpion as tall as himself.

"I mean you no harm," he said, sliding his hand over the pommel of the sword beneath his cloak. "Allow me to pass. I seek an audience with your mistress."

The monster raised its stinger and snapped its pincers, which gave off a bone-crunching sound. With the training of Achilles embedded in his astral body, a plan formed before Julien could even register it as such. He withdrew his sword and raised it high above his head in false intention, bounded forward and leapt early, feinting a downward thrust upon the beast's head. The scorpion reared up and snatched with its claws as Julien landed, rolled, and lunged from the ground. He thrusted at the chitinous opening just below the creature's head, but no sooner had he felt the penetrating access of his sword, cracking its way through the carapace, than the creature dissolved into light and disappeared.

It was merely a mirage, Julien realized as he rose to his feet. But it had still been a trial—and one he had passed. He approached the cave door and pierced the ankh-shaped keyhole with his sword. He heard the sound of a latch releasing, followed by an outburst of acrid air as the hermetically sealed door swung open. Julien sheathed his sword and advanced down a torchlit hallway until he reached a large chamber, where the air had turned from acrid to pungent and he could sense the presence of an active intelligence.

A viscous light began to glow in the center of the chamber, just like that which had taken the form of the scorpion. "What do I look like?" the light spoke in vibrations, as if strummed on an ancient instrument.

Julien presented his two hands, palms forward, with his slender fingers splayed. He manipulated his digits as though tickling the ivories of a piano, and projected from his mind the phantasm of the feminine ideal he beheld in Pygmalion's studio before Eros had appeared.

The light became aroused and appeared to dance. "Seduce me with your words, poet," it commanded.

"Between your legs lies what you believe to be your burden," Julien intoned. "Scorpio is the sign of sex, but there is also more love in it than in the eleven others combined. The Supreme Author, your creator, has concentrated to the highest and most volatile degree between your legs the power of dark devotion, yet you have no one to give it to, for no one is worthy of such a love. You pine for a hero who offers himself completely, for with you love is everything or nothing."

"How would you love me?" asked the light.

"You wish to be bound by your own beauty," said Julien, "which is why I would take your raven tresses and weave them into a tight bun, symbolic of your coiled powers. Then I would wrap you in a corset that enhances your figure with artistry, prominently displaying your breasts. Against your loins I would strap the finest silk, which is wedged between your buttocks as a constant annoyance of arousal. Then, through this veil of silk separating your sex from the outside world, I would inhale your elixir as if it were the ether itself while, on the other side of the veil, you marinate in your own arousal, in the knowledge that someone has found and venerated the power between your legs."

The light ceased its dancing form and became agitated.

"Then I would mount you from behind," Julien continued. "Your obsession is penetration, so I would enter your dark and forbidden passage, and the validation of this passage would drive you to delirium. Your front would quiver while remaining untouched, for with you agony and ecstasy are the same. I would hover my chin over your shoulder and behold the beauty of your face in pleasure, but our mouths would not yet kiss. Instead we would take in each other's breath until waves of crescendo had shaken you to the core. At last I would penetrate your mouth with my tongue, swallowing your muffled moans."

"Enough!" the light said in a powerful female voice. "I shall coalesce before you as your womanly ideal and flood you with all the smells of incarnation: perfume and perspiration, tawny hair, the musk of my front passage, and the oud of my back. And you will be unable to bear it, your quest will fail, you will tumble into limbo!"

The empty cave evaporated, revealing the light's true home: a palace of stunning opulence. Then the light coalesced into a perfection Julien had never known, so oddly distinct was this feminine beauty. Clad in a flowing black gown, Aphrodite Scorpia fixed Julien with a riveting gaze, waved her hand, and sent invisible clouds of fragrant elixir toward him. Julien steadily advanced, Aphrodite trembled, and in a moment she was wrapped in his arms. Instinctively she sought to free herself, but Julien brushed her cheek with his fingertips and kissed the top of her forehead where it met her bound hair.

"You are meant to be loved, not feared," he said, "dark lady of my dreams, muse of my anguished art."

"I've waited for eons," Aphrodite said, her eyes moist.

Julien took her hand. "We are needed."

Aphrodite pulled him towards the inner sanctum of her palace. "Stay with me here," she said. "Love me."

"You cannot stay locked away," countered Julien. "Don't you see? You're no longer in your detriment."

Aphrodite explained that Olympus had fallen, and she did not know where the other gods had fled. She only ever convened with them when the wheel in the sky turned to the sign of Scorpio and she had no choice.

"The wheel has turned," said Julien. "You had the ankh keyhole and I the sword-key. You're not sterile anymore. We have re-forged the bond between gods and men, but my mission is not complete."

"I know," sighed Aphrodite. "Spoken like one of Zeus's true heroes for the Age of Iron. I cannot leave this place, but my will is sovereign. I shall extract a drop of my essence and create the muse you have seen in your dreams. She will be your occult bride and my proxy, with her own free will and light from my intelligence, albeit in keeping with her lesser station. Shall we call her Lena, which in Hellas means light?"

"Let us call her Darlena," said Julien, "for she has been my dark light."

Aphrodite Scorpia dissolved back into divine light. Then, with a flash of lightning, she generated a new being, and before Julien stood a feminine form even more beautiful than the deity, for it aroused the sentimental part of him that still carried earthly ties. Julien's occult bride was clad in tight shorts of black leather and a sleeveless black sheer tunic of sumptuous fabric, through which her perfectly formed breasts were visible. Her sandals were leather with black satin ribbon wrapped up to her knees in the highest achievement of the couturier's art. On her upper arms she wore golden bands of Aegyptian design, yet her hair was piled high like a Parisian lady of fashion, and her lips were painted scarlet.

When the pair exited the cavern and crossed the Valley of the Queens, Darlena spoke her first words. "We have far to travel, my love," she said. "Have you come by Pegasus? Or would you like me to arrange our journey? For in ancient times Scorpio was also symbolized by the eagle."

Julien replied that he had something else in mind. "How much have you seen of earth's future?" he asked.

"Very little," Darlena replied. "I stopped looking when I saw what was happening."

"Then you don't know what a motorcar is?"

"By the sound of it," Darlena scoffed, "I can tell it has nothing to do with sex or beauty."

"I wouldn't be so sure about that," said Julien as they exited the canyon, pointing at the Diablo shining in the moonlight.

Darlena tilted her head, her imagination clearly aroused, and walked slowly towards the machine. Julien raised the gull-wing doors, revealing the cognac-colored leather inside. Darlena laughed at how cramped it was and called it absurd, but Julien helped her in and fired up the engine, reminding Darlena how much Scorpio loved power. At first the thunderous sound irked her, but when Julien put the motorcar in gear, spun around, and accelerated northbound at full throttle, she fell back in her seat with a look of terrified fascination.

Then, knowing how much she loved dramatic contrasts, Julien pressed the magic musical button, filling the cabin with the strains of Chausson's "*Poème*." Darlena began pawing herself, clutching her breasts, stroking her thighs, and squirming in her seat. With a devilish smile Julien encouraged her, so she raised her sandaled feet to the dash, spread her legs, and slid her hand down her shorts, moaning in harmony with the agony of the violin.

When the ecstasy was finished the pair shared an embarrassed laugh, then settled silently into the long drive, each gazing out the window at the starlit sky and vast desert. As the miles rolled by they glanced at each other coyly, until, halfway up the Nile, their gazes met in mutual longing.

"Doesn't it go any faster?" Darlena complained.

There were 200 miles left before they reached the Scorpitaria, where they would be able to melt into their own world deep beneath the sea. Julien culled even more velocity from the motorcar's roaring engine, before suddenly changing his mind and slamming the brakes. The machine came to a dead halt, surrounded by its own dust storm. Darlena needed no assistance in climbing out of the vehicle, and the two rushed into each other's arms. Julien bent Darlena over the front of the Diablo, sank to his knees, and pulled down her shorts, unveiling the sacred geometry of her backside.

"What's this?" she muttered.

"The face of God," Julien replied, kissing her buttocks.

Darlena reached behind, grabbed Julien's hair, and yanked him to his feet. She pointed to the gap line running around the front of the machine, speculating that it must be some kind of compartment. Julien climbed back inside the Diablo, found the proper button, and pressed it, causing Darlena to motion excitedly. Julien climbed back out, slid his fingers under the dislodged gap, and raised the door. This secret compartment contained no riddles hidden in books, only a card depicting a heart, signed Eros. Beneath it rested a mink fur and two cushions — one embroidered with a golden sword, the other with a golden ankh — which the lovers took to the bank of the river, where they sealed their bond in a purple flowerbed of Lily of the Nile.

When they resumed their journey and the pyramids came into view, Darlena cried out in joy. Soon after they reached the Nile basin, where Julien returned the Diablo to the grotto where he had found it. And as the mysteries of the Supreme Creator were as enchanting to Darlena as they were to Julien, the pair watched in wonder as the "sexy beast" of the future dissolved back into the ether from which it had materialized. When the last twinkles of magic dust had evaporated, they found a note lying on the ground:

Julien and Darlena:

Triangulate the islands of Bellikos, Aesthtikos, and Erotikos, and you will find the resting place of fallen Olympus.

Love and art are only possible if war makes peace, and the armies of darkness are defeated.

Ever Faithfully Yours,

Eros

The couple swam to the Scorpitaria and Julien spoke the destination into the navigation shell. When he turned around, he discovered that Darlena had already put her aesthetic powers to use. Having exhausted their purpose, the heroic scenes on the ship's walls had been replaced with violet damask, and the floor was now covered in black carpeting. Inspired by Eros's gesture in the Diablo, Darlena had also replaced the animal hides with furs of mink and sable, and added five velvet cushions. As the ship embarked for Hellas, she removed her garments and lay inside the love nest she had made, shooting Julien a look that was both an invitation and a challenge.

Drawn by the vibrations escaping from the Scorpitaria, a school of mermaids soon came to watch the lovers through the portholes. Because of her kinship to Ares through the sign of Scorpio, Darlena's lovemaking reminded Julien of his grappling in the Basin of Adonis. He would dominate her, forcing her into the receptive state, whereupon she would alter her polarity to the active state, trying to force Julien to the point of release. The only way in which Darlena could feel truly herself was through this struggling fusion, in which her energy was matched by a reciprocal one, as if her lover was both a partner and opponent.

Julien soon understood that in his earthly matings he and his paramours had sought to melt into one another, each seeking the missing piece needed for completion. But he had climbed the spiral staircase of initiation to master the Royal Art, and now possessed the double-serpent as part of his nature. Born of a deity, Darlena also possessed the quintessence energy, and when their two double-serpent currents came into contact—with attraction and repulsion firing simultaneously, and their individual beings maintained—their theurgic lovemaking made possible the creation of new currents in the Astral Light.

Yet behind Darlena's ferocious sexual energy was the most loyal devotion, a tremendous compassion for the suffering and injustice Julien had endured, and an incredible capacity for healing. She was indeed Julien's soulmate, his muse and guide for navigating the end of the world. While they rested, she asked him to speak to her as though she were one of his earthly lovers. Cuddling her in his arms, Julien recounted the journey that had led him to the present moment. Darlena was deeply moved, then deeply troubled, revealing that she bore a painful warning concerning the next stage of his quest and his eventual return to the underworld.

"Without war, without noble kings commanding warriors like Achilles, there can be no beauty, no art, no music, no voluptuousness," she said. "The faceless multitudes, the principle of darkness, the dream-killers, the ugly and ignorant — they are insatiable in their appetite for destruction, like a black hole in the heavens that sucks and destroys anything it comes near."

Leaning onto his elbow, Julien asked what she was trying to tell him.

"I'm trying to say that without heroes, we — that is, all who serve Aphrodite — cannot exert our influence. Love between men and women shall slowly perish, and a black shroud of death will fall across Europa, permitting the land to be invaded by her enemies. There's no story without good and evil, day and night, summer and winter, a land that blooms like a rose and then crumbles to the wind. Europa will become a tragic wasteland, more desolate than you can imagine. And all the world will assist in her self-destruction, for such is the way of the cosmos according to the Supreme Author. There must be a story, victors and the vanquished. The Hyperborean cycle is closing, my love, but the Royal Art prepares kings for other realms."

Julien stared at the ceiling, whereupon sunlight began to shine through the ship's portholes. He rose and began to dress, but Darlena stopped him. As the Scorpitaria came to rest on the ocean's surface, she opened the hatch and pulled herself, unclothed, on top of the ship. After surveying the sky and sea, she said through the opening that the coordinates were correct. There was a temple of Poseidon beneath them to which they must swim. Julien climbed up to join her.

As the Olympians were made of *prima materia* and ruled the four elements, Darlena explained, there would be sufficient air for Julien to breathe inside the temple. In order to reach it, she would bestow upon him a magic kiss filled with the breath of eternity. They would arrive at the temple in a state of absolute nakedness, she continued, and she would coalesce proper attire upon their arrival. Julien nodded, Darlena kissed him, and they dove into the sea.

No sooner had they begun their incursion into the depths than the mermaids appeared. Having watched the lovers with reverence and felt their generative power, the water-maidens had followed the Scorpitaria from Aegyptus and gestured an offer of assistance. Julien and Darlena each took hold of two mermaids, grabbing onto their waists, and the creatures of wonder sped through the deepening shades of blue as the light of Apollo grew dim.

But soon a new light appeared: Greek fire. Two lights glowed at the bottom of the sea, and as the mermaids pulled Julien closer, he detected two urns burning a form of magic flame impervious to water, which flanked a cave entrance above which was carved the trident of Poseidon. The mermaids dispersed with a nod of divine kinship, and Julien and Darlena swam the remaining strokes through the opening, surfacing in a small pool inside a dank chamber, their wet bodies drying instantaneously in the light of more magic torches.

Darlena waved her hand and Julien felt himself being clothed in black leather breeches, tall boots, and a flowing white shirt, which opened over his chest to reveal the bronze musculature he had earned over the course of his quest. Darlena also summoned for him a princely cloak with the Scorpitarian clasp, altered to a regal midnight shade of blue. Then Julien's sword coalesced at his side, housed in a sheath that had been polished to the mirror finish of a grand piano, attached to a belt of violet suede.

Before Darlena could attire herself they heard the sound of footsteps. At the end of a long hallway stood a figure of imposing stature, wearing armor and a red cloak that brushed the ground. Darlena stroked Julien's arm reassuringly, then walked in her divine nudity down the length of the corridor in the magic torchlight. After exchanging greetings with Ares she pivoted, the god of war following behind while admiring her form. She returned to Julien's side and made the appropriate introductions.

Julien had earned his place in the dimension where gods and men worked in communion, and his bearing was the epitome of poise. He bowed with measured respect to the great god, whose haggard and scarred aspect was not unlike Julien's own at the outset of his adventure.

After Darlena asked who else was present, Ares explained that The Twelve had not convened for a very long time and lived mostly in solitude, exerting their influence as best they could. Although the temple was Poseidon's home, he had journeyed to the frigid waters of the North Atlantic. "Men have launched the largest ship ever built, which they named for the Titans," said Ares, "and Poseidon has arranged an iceberg to show man the destiny that awaits him as a result of his profane exploits in industry and enterprise. As for myself, I have the ignominious task of filling the hearts of the nobility with courage for the coming war, that they may slaughter each other and bring an end to the aristocracy. Only Zeus is here, and spends his time brooding upon his throne. I take it you wish to have an audience with him?"

Julien and Darlena nodded, and Ares proceeded to lead them down the corridor and through a vast hall where the only sound was water trickling down the stone walls. Their path ended at a pair of tall doors. Ares asked the pair to wait while he spoke to the King of the Gods. A moment later the doors opened and Ares ushered them inside.

Zeus sat upon a raised throne at the center of a royal chamber of grandiose austerity. He wore a black robe with a pointed collar framing his imposing visage, which was set off by a diamond-shaped beard and mustachios curled upwards. His posture was weary but defiant, and perked up at the sight of his beautiful female visitor.

Darlena approached the throne with utmost grace, took Zeus's hand, and bestowed upon it an affectionate kiss. "Great Lord, I am called Darlena," she said. "I was conceived in Aegyptus by Aphrodite Scorpia, who made me the bride of this great hero, who fights for the Primordial Tradition in the Age of Iron. She decreed that I should act as her proxy until such time that the gods convene once again, and the stars turn to her time."

Zeus nodded in acknowledgement, then turned his eyes to Julien. "Is this the hero I sired at the castle in Gaul?"

Julien did not hesitate, for he who hesitates is lost. He had heard the Truth with a capital T, and bounded up the seven steps to Zeus's throne, falling to his knees. "Father," he sobbed.

The Lord of the Gods stroked Julien's hair with an affection so deep that his thunderous power emanated from Poseidon's undersea temple, causing waves to crash on all the islands of Elysium. From there the force descended in a spiral through the Great Chain of Being, and a sudden rainstorm fell across the continent of Europa.

What ensued was a colloquy the heavens had not heard for many eons, as mortal and deities reasoned, strategized, and used every spark of divine intelligence with which they had been bestowed in an effort to halt the decline of the European races, who were on a path that would lead them to submit in shame to tyrannical leaders and savage invaders. Darlena pleaded, Ares paced, and Julien listened with composure fortified by determination. But Zeus concluded that, according to laws written by the Supreme Author long before their time, there was nothing the gods of Mount Olympus could do until they had been awakened in enough men's hearts, as they had in Julien's, prompting the hero to ask how many would be enough.

"When do buds burst forth in spring?" laughed Zeus. "When does a boy become a man? When the time comes."

Julien nodded solemnly, accepting that he would be forced to live through the decadence, and that it would be well past his time when Europa passed the negative limit and its men suddenly remembered who they were. However, Zeus and Ares cautioned, there was no guarantee this would ever happen, for it was the nature of the future to remain unwritten. The Hyperborean race could very well go extinct on the face of the earth, surviving only in the Astral Light with the aid of those souls called to tend the perennial fire.

"Now you must go back to your world, my dear Julien," said Zeus, "for you were entrusted with a mission, and others await your return."

"But my mission failed," said Julien.

"No, it has succeeded gloriously. It is other men who have failed. But it is not your fault that men are fools, forgetting the things that are good and noble, and forsaking the gods."

Julien asked whether he would ever see him again, to which Zeus responded with an ambiguous gaze. In tacit understanding Julien nodded and began to exit with Darlena, while Ares climbed the steps and stood beside Zeus on his throne.

When the couple reached the tall doors, Ares called out to Julien and said that while it was Eros who had led him through the Mysteries, and Aphrodite who had helped him find the temple of Poseidon, the God of War ruled Julien's soul through the Sun placement in his natal chart. "Therefore, upon your return to the land of men," he said, "know that you have all my powers at your disposal, and that I command Achilles and his myrmidons."

Julien said he was honored and grateful, and watched as the two deities suddenly stared at him with swords in their eyes.

"There is something you could do, my son," said Zeus. "A symbolic act, but one that would echo across the land and even resound in the heavens."

"Name it, father," replied Julien, "and it will be done."

Zeus and Ares shared a cold glance before voicing their command in unison:

"Kill the bitch."

CHAPTER TEN

IT WAS COMPLETELY dark save for the amber glow of the Scorpitaria's circuitry. The ship was silent, and Julien sensed that he had returned to Zapfe's studio in the Venetian lagoon. All his earthly memories came tumbling into his mind like an avalanche. He was a fugitive from justice, wanted for the assassination of the King of Gaul, and had no place to call home. But he also recalled every detail of his Hellenic journey, including his sad farewell to Darlena, for she could not accompany him to terrestrial reality, and vowed to remain in the temple of Poseidon.

Julien roused himself, shaking his head in disbelief at the details of his lucid dream. Whatever was in the philter Zapfe had given him, it had conjured images more outlandish than the opium-fueled hallucinations in Berlioz's *Symphonie Fantastique.* He was comfortably ensconced in the submersible watercraft's love-nest of fur and velvet, and recalled how the walls had once depicted heroic scenes before Darlena had beautified the ship with violet damask. Noting his fine attire, Julien surmised that decorators from the opera had costumed him and redesigned the set of the Scorpitaria, but how had they known what he had seen? Had Zapfe programmed his visions with magic? Had the magus — perhaps even Zoe — been watching Julien the whole time in the Astral Light?

Through the portholes he saw no sign of a greeting party. Grabbing his knapsack, Julien cinched the cloak over his shoulder and notched the sword-belt around his waist. He climbed out of the hatch, leapt onto the platform running along the canal, and ascended the steps toward a light, which he discovered was not a candle, but a flickering Edison bulb.

Gone were all the devices of Zapfe and his robed brotherhood, and the lone piece of furniture was the table where the magus had helped Julien solve the riddle of Pygmalion. A white envelope bearing his name lay upon it. Inside Julien found a stack of notes in a currency he did not recognize, and a slip of paper on which was written "Hotel Ulisse" with a cryptic set of numbers.

Julien made his way up the main staircase through the dank building, kicking rats along the way until he could finally throw open the door, see by the moonlight, and breathe the Venetian night air. The island of Poveglia was as desolate as he remembered it, but a gondola sat at the edge of the water as though waiting for him. As Julien rowed it towards the Lido, the feeling of bobbing on the water flooded his mind with thoughts of Darlena and their voyage through the Aegean, but his reveries were interrupted by the sound of cannon fire and explosions lighting up the sky.

Julien's first thought was that the world was at war but, when several more blasts erupted in colorful lights above the city, followed by roars of revelry, Julien concluded that it was simply the season of the *Carnevale*, a serendipity that only higher powers could have arranged. A wanted man did not need the authorities stopping him to ask why he was carrying a sword, and the cloak hid the weapon perfectly. Julien kept his hand on the pommel to steady its sway as he exited the gondola and made his way through the city.

If the crowd's costumes were lewd, their behavior was even more so, as though the streets were one giant Satanic orgy. There was open-air fellatio and lecherous couplings against buildings while onlookers abused themselves in the shadows. Having tasted divine love, Julien turned up his nose in disgust at what he saw. But with the labyrinthine design of the city-on-water, he was forced to constantly ask directions from drunken revelers, who struck him as scarcely human.

When he reached the Hotel Ulisse he found it was not the rotting *pensione* of before. Some investor had come in and spruced up the painted harlot. There was not a room available anywhere in Venice, the pretentious concierge informed him, but they had kept a reservation for a Mr. Stanwyck on the promise that he would pay triple the usual *Carnevale* rate. Julien produced the envelope of bills and told the man to take all he wanted—a wish his interlocutor was happy to oblige. Then Julien asked whether the numbers on the slip of paper he had brought had any particular meaning.

"They look like a telephone number, sir," the concierge replied. "Germanic lands, from what I can tell."

Julien smiled awkwardly in an effort to hide his ignorance, whereupon the concierge pointed across the lobby at an open booth hung with a curtain. With the sword under his cloak Julien climbed awkwardly inside and assessed the invention. As he placed the receiver to his ear, he thought fondly of the magic seashell inside the Scorpitaria. A moment later a female voice asked for the number to which he wished to be connected. Julien read off the series of digits on the paper, and was instructed to "stand by" as he was connected to the Swiss Republic.

There were so many things to demand of Zapfe, starting with an answer as to why there had been no one to welcome his return. While he waited, he pondered the word "telephone," breaking down its roots to "far sound," and remembered back in New York reading about the invention of a certain Alexander Graham Bell.

The female voice returned to Julien's ear, telling him to "go ahead," whereupon he heard another voice that was clearly not Zapfe's.

"Zoe?" Julien all but shouted.

"Yes!"

"I can't believe it. This device. Hearing you. It's pure magic!"

"And listen to you," said Zoe, "sounding every bit the 'happy magical hero' of the Renaissance text. Do you know what 'happy' means in this context?"

Julien said no, but that there was one person who would, and she was probably about to tell him.

"It means succeeding in an adventure," laughed Zoe. "And you were successful, I take it."

Julien said that he had made contact with the old gods through the wonder-workings of theurgy, but did not understand why Zapfe was not in Poveglia to greet him. Zoe informed him that Zapfe was dead.

"Of what?" asked Julien. "He was so full of vitality."

"Old age."

Julien fell silent.

Zoe took a deep breath. "Julien, it's 1919. You've been gone 20 years."

Julien remained speechless as Zoe filled him in on the developments in the realm of Becoming, or what humans called "history." There had been a great war, revolutions, and the demise of the aristocracy. A man named Spengler had just published a book called *Decline of the West.* Most of Europa's kingdoms had become republics, albeit in name only. "The modern masses look like people as you remember them," she said, "but they're not the same. We call them gogs. They are purely material beings, their minds programmed by their corrupt societies. They do not have souls."

Julien mentioned having been warned of such things, which had now evidently come to pass. Zoe told him the evil which had sprouted up at the close of the 19th century was far worse than anything they had imagined, prompting Julien to inquire how she spent her time.

"I do what I can," she sighed, "organizing, writing, synthesizing, preserving the story of our people..."

"Who's there with you?"

"A few vassals. The others — Zapfe's coterie of guardians — have all fled. Some wanted to die a warrior's death, others took a book and disappeared, so as to disperse the preservation of the Tradition."

Julien said he would be joining her shortly, but Zoe told him to wait, asking whether he remembered the Tarot spread she had done for him on their voyage to the Old World. Julien said he would never forget it, and Zoe asked whether he knew where he was now.

"I think so," replied Julien. "It started with the Death of my mother, then I met a Priestess in you, encountered the Catastrophe of Europa, became a Hermit and fugitive, and found Love in the astral realm. That leaves the Devil and the Emperor."

"Good. Then you know what destiny demands of you."

"I know because Zeus told me himself: he wants Regina Grossman dead."

"As do I," said Zoe. She proceeded to explain that Regina Grossman, now Empress of Gaul, had seized Julien's château to serve as the headquarters of her empire. "The village of Tour-Abolie is much changed, with large concrete buildings erected for her staff. But they've left the tavern for nostalgia's sake. I'll send someone there who can help you find a way into the château, which is heavily guarded. You understand the power of invisibility?"

"To be invisible is to be undetected," replied Julien.

"Precisely," said Zoe. "With cunning and guile you'll find a way in. Today is Saturday. Let's plan for Tuesday, since it's named for Mars, the god of war. Be at the tavern at 9 pm, and may the gods be with you."

In his room Julien threw off his cloak and unhitched his sword. Although he had awakened just two hours earlier, he felt exhausted and planned to catch an early train. When he went to bathe, the bathroom evoked memories of the waterfall at the Basin of Adonis, for the water came showering down from a mounting on the wall. Julien wrestled with the plumbing until the water came from below, filling the tub in the familiar way. Then he tore off his shirt and removed his boots and breeches, and just as he was about to climb into the steaming water he thought he saw a ghost.

Julien's reflection in the mirror showed the definition in his arms and legs he had earned under the tutelage of Achilles, the power in his chest and shoulders from grappling, and the bronzing from the Hellenic sun. There was a gentle light in his eyes from his time spent with the sapphic women and hermaphrodites, and a plushness to his lips.

But Aegyptus had aged him.

His golden-streaked chestnut locks were now gray, and his chiseled face was covered with a hoary beard that flowed in ringlets, radiant with vigor and glistening with precious oils. With his mustache swept rakishly aside, he looked part Grecian philosopher-king, part Gothic lord in a castle lined with suits of armor—in other words, every bit the image of his father Zeus, whose thunderbolt had sired him that night in the Château de la Tour-Abolie.

Julien slid into the hot bath as his mind went to work. The philter Zapfe had given him must have rendered him unconscious. He had been taken to Hellas to study and train, and constantly fed the hypnotic potion, which guided his visions. So in a certain way the phantasmagoria that had swept across the Old World had gotten him, too. Julien had succumbed to the hauntings of his own mind, and all his soul's obsessions had played out through the Universal Plastic Medium, his imagination, as it existed within the imagination of the Supreme Author.

But Julien soon ceased this line of reasoning, moving from everyday logic to occult wisdom. "All truths are but half-truths," he said to himself, "for the opposite is also true." In one way or another he had left the world and spent 20 years in the numinal dimension of consciousness, and was now a seasoned man of 47 with a body primed for war, a spirit schooled in magic, and direct orders from fallen Olympus.

The city was silent in the early hours, with only the detritus of the night's orgies on the foggy streets of Venice as Julien made his way to the station at Santa Lucia, sack over his shoulder and sword under his arm, which he had wrapped in the cloak and tied with twine. He spent the next two days on trains, taking the Swiss route from Milano rather than the southern line through Lyon. His fellow travelers were like soulless wraiths: hardly interacting, clothing drab, their heads bowed and eyes vacant. When they did turn their attention to something it was invariably a newspaper, which filled their receptive minds with whatever the editors wished. And whenever Julien peered out the window he felt only heartbreak at the gird-iron skeletons of concrete-slab buildings being erected, as though Europa were about to become an enormous penal colony.

He arrived in Paris on the morning of the third day. With motorcars for hire everywhere — comically ugly compared to the Diablo he had piloted through Aegyptus — it would be a short trip to La Tour-Abolie, leaving Julien the entire day to revisit his old haunts.

The city was crowded with people scurrying about, so unlike the boulevardiers of old, who elegantly drifted in unhurried appreciation of the city's pleasures. Ladies had cut their hair and wore shapeless silhouettes, while the gentlemen had shed their rakish beards and waxed mustachios, and dressed in suits that made them look not gentlemanly, but bureaucratic. Julien soon found himself in the Latin Quarter, standing before the building where he had once lived.

A young man emerged covered with paint and carrying a canvas; Julien stopped him and said that he had once lived in the top-floor studio. When the man replied that this was the very unit where he lived, Julien politely inquired about the price of letting there. The sum was so astonishing that he could hardly believe it. But it was evidently no trouble for the young painter, who was rushing the fresh canvas to a gallery, where demand outpaced supply. Julien asked to see the work and the young man proudly displayed the painting, which looked like something a dog had regurgitated.

"A work of genius, if I may say so."

"You may," the artist replied proudly. "Everyone else does."

Julien next made his way to Chat Noir, only to find the establishment had shut down. The Moulin Rouge was still open, but it had become a caricature of its former glory, catering to ignorant tourists for whom the *Belle Époque* was as spiritually distant as the Middle Ages. Julien found a cafe and sat outside on the bustling boulevard, but the atmosphere was not one of gaiety and wit, and the conversations he overheard at nearby tables only confirmed that he belonged to a world that no longer existed.

When dusk fell, he hired a taxicab to take him to La Tour-Abolie, where his rude awakening only continued: the monstrous metropolis of Paris had absorbed outlying villages like some cancerous growth, gobbling acreage and erecting cement ant-farms where the new breed of human lived and worked. But it was in his own rightful village that he witnessed the horror of what two decades of wormwood mind-poisoning had done. The driver left him at a busy thoroughfare, the tavern surrounded by apartment buildings for sycophants who served the empress.

Julien took a seat by the old fireplace, which had been replaced by an electric lamp that imitated the flickering of fire. The Reynards were no longer the proprietors, and the patrons were the logical conclusion of everything Julien had witnessed that day in Paris. The diners were mostly women, all of them overweight and dressed in some kind of deliberate affront to standards of beauty. Vibrationally speaking, they were human embodiments of the Devil's Interval, a fatuous anti-energy, a kind of black hole that negated anything containing a positive polarity charge. They stuck jewelry in their noses like the sirens on that horrendous night in Hellas, and, like those grotesque fish-women, had covered their portly bodies in seaweed-colored tattoos.

A man took a seat, waking Julien from his brooding. He wore a serious look and said he had been sent to assist Julien with his mission. Julien asked if the man was aware of the dangers. The stranger nodded, and Julien coldly inquired how he might be of help.

"Julien, do you really not recognize me? It's me, Maurice LeBlanc."

Julien's heart leapt at the revelation of the only mortal friend he had ever known. Gone was the introspective but audacious artist from their cabaret collaboration, replaced by a well seasoned man who had also sought to penetrate the veil of Mystery.

"And look at you," said Maurice affectionately. "From Byronic troubadour to true nobleman."

With bittersweet verve Maurice revealed to Julien all that had transpired while he was away, telling him how Europa had succumbed to subversion by the merchant and servant castes, replacing kingdoms with so-called democracies that controlled the ignorant masses with top-down corruption. Regina Grossman, as the Duchess of Fontaine-Sombre, had slipped like a snake between the worlds of finance, nobility, and the proletariat to rise in the world of politics. After the Great War she was elected Prime Minister under anti-male sentiment stemming from the futility of the conflict. Then, avowing that men could no longer be trusted, she had declared herself Empress of Gaul and was busy replacing history with falsehoods and celebrations of communal life — matriarchal tyranny from above and chaos from below.

Satanarchy was what they called it, Maurice explained. Drawing with his finger on the table, he showed Julien the associated symbol:

```
  A
  N
  A
  R
  C
  H
  I
  S
SATAN
  I
  C
```

The required escape for those fighting the occult war was a leap from the horizontal realm of Becoming to the vertical dimension of Being, and looked like this:

```
   T
   R
   A
   N
   S
   C
   E
   N
DECADENCE
   E
   N
   C
   E
```

"After you left," Maurice continued, "I returned to my studies of the Primordial Tradition that was suppressed during the Christian era.

The path led me to magic, and eventually to theurgy. But I lacked the heroic qualifications, and when I had reached my limit, with no way to halt the dissolution, I retired to a quiet life as a family man and music teacher in Normandy. But the number of students dwindles each year, and those who remain only want to learn dissonance, never harmony. The art of today is one of negation: taking an established form and making it ugly. You never did that. Your music was always powered by truth and beauty, you just did it darkly. Never did you say to yourself, 'How can I make the world uglier and more chaotic?'"

Julien wanted to know how far he had gotten with theurgy, and Maurice replied that he had reached the border of the overworld, but had not been able to enter into conjunction. "That's when I accepted that I could only be a guardian of the ancient wisdom, a priest but not a king. But you actually entered and acted within the Astral Light?"

"I went through initiation along the Way of Sex," said Julien matter of factly, "which led me to the frequency where the gods of Hellas still live. I entered union with fallen Olympus and was awarded an occult bride made of spirit called Darlena, for she is my dark light."

Maurice inspected Julien's cuffs and meditated upon their symbolism. He said that Julien was backed by divine justice, for the château was rightfully his, and that Regina was powered by the force of destruction. "Although evil is currently ascendant, it is nevertheless the secondary force," he explained. "Goodness, light, creation and the masculine are the first principle; evil, destruction, night, and the feminine are the second. What the double-serpents on these cuffs express to me is the doctrine that draws a secret distinction between good and evil, light and dark. There are active and passive energies, and then there's the polarity of creation and destruction. Dark energy can serve divine light, just as the active light of intelligence can create evil."

Julien praised Maurice's wisdom, but said they would need a plan of action to infiltrate the castle.

Everything to the east had been absorbed by Paris, Maurice informed him, and the old road leading through the valley and up the hill was fenced and guarded. "But the west side—do you remember when you fled after the king's assassination? That's still forest, where your estate borders Regina's, and is probably our best point of entry. There will no doubt be barriers, and her inner sanctum is guarded by witches. But I have an idea: do you like cats?"

"You know I adore cats," Julien replied, "as did Poe, Baudelaire, Barbey d'Aurevilly, our friend Robert de Montesquiou, and every other kindred spirit."

"Exactly," said Maurice, growing crafty as a plan began to hatch. "Cats are lodged in our imaginations, giving them potency, and they sneak about undetected under the veil of night—especially black ones."

"I see where you're going," said Julien mercurially. "And did we not gain our notoriety at Chat Noir? And was not our first collaboration in that very castle, playing games with only the piano and the power of make-believe?"

The friends shared a laugh over the memory that they had once said, "Fun, what's that?" Now they knew that magic was the most fun thing in the world, especially—and tragically—when facing the end of the world. The men continued ruminating, while supernatural forces of the numen guided and shaped their thoughts.

"In my study of theurgic invocations," ventured Maurice, "part of the lore I encountered is the power consecrated objects have to summon forces through the Astral Light. I may be able to invoke powers of 'invisibility'—or the ability to pass undetected, as though a higher power has cleared our way—if we had some kind of charm or talisman."

"Why not my cuffs?" said Julian.

Maurice cocked his head in amazement, whereupon Julien clarified that he had indeed brought them back from the overworld, where they had undergone a progressive transformation. Maurice pronounced them divine amulets, saying that Julien possessed consecrated magic right at his fingertips, through the very hands by which he had made his artistic creations.

Julien said that another feline power resided in the claws of cats, waving his hands with fingers arched like daggers, pantomiming powers of light that would cause the enemy to bleed out. Maurice deemed it brilliant, but Julien said he had an even better talisman, and beneath the table unwrapped the end of his cloak, revealing the pommel of the sword of Achilles.

Stunned that it had passed through the ether to re-coagulate in earthly reality, Maurice was convinced that any magical act utilizing it would be successful. "Timing and location will be key. There should be two stages: the Black Cat invocation to infiltrate the estate, and the Sword of Achilles to get us to the empress."

The men exited the tavern amid stares, as men of their demeanor were seldom seen in the community surrounding Empress Regina. They proceeded north for a mile to an entrance into the woodland, then began climbing the hill eastward amid the sounds of the night. When they reached the deepest part of the forest they stopped at the base of a tree of exceptional configuration, an arboreal sentinel whose vibrations, said Maurice, would strengthen their resolve and aid in the success of their endeavor.

He rummaged through his coat pockets and withdrew matches, candles, and his own grimoire, compiled from 25 years of study. Julien unwrapped the sword, tied the belt around his waist, donned his cloak, and bequeathed his weathered rucksack to his friend to carry the supplies. Maurice lit a candle and sought an appropriate passage by the light of the flaming wax.

When he found the right words he nodded, commenced the ritual, and he and Julien entered the active trance state of *mag*. They imagined what they willed and willed what they imagined: namely, that they would draw power through the ether which would keep them undetected, at which point Zeus would provide bolts of light which

Julien would propel through his hands via his serpent cuffs, causing lacerations to their enemies and fatality by blood loss. These were the rites of their divine mission and the act of magic they called Black Cat, because of the role this symbol played in their personal destinies. When they returned to everyday consciousness, each beheld in his fellow's eyes a complete command over the intelligent faculties, to which they had added the feline power of silent movement and razor-sharp beams of claw light.

Continuing their ascent through the forest, their footsteps on the brittle leaves barely registered a sound above the nocturnal chorus of birds and insects. When the forest ended an open field appeared separating the two estates, with Le Château de la Fontaine-Sombre to the left and Le Château de la Tour-Abolie to the right. While light shone through several of Regina's windows, there were far more glowing lights at Julien's estate. The pair shared a nod and made their approach.

They were soon met by a wall Regina had installed around La Tour-Abolie. It was not made of stone, which would have been in harmony with the Medieval architecture, but jagged wood. Despite the dangerous spikes and threat of making noise, Julien and Maurice scaled the wall in silence, dropping on the other side as though they had pads on the soles of their boots.

Scurrying through the shadows to stay out of the moonlight, they soon discerned the eccentric nature of Regina's barrier. She had renovated the château's garden not with roses and marble, but with sticks and bones gathered in crude forms. Meanwhile, the fountain featured a bloated female figure holding misshapen teats from which black water slowly dripped.

Guards patrolled the grounds, but their pattern was irregular. They wandered randomly, stopping periodically to practice strange nocturnal rituals, hailing the moon, prancing momentarily like demons, then yawning and resuming their walk. With an exchange barely above the level of a purring cat, Julien and Maurice vowed to avoid the genderless gendarmes at all costs, slipping from shadow to shadow towards the castle's rear entrance.

They stopped against the wall of the old tower, which Julien, in all the accelerated madness of his short tenure as lord of the manor, had never investigated. He motioned to Maurice, pointing to his nose and making a sniffing gesture. Maurice nodded agreement, remembering the noxious aroma they had smelled decades before. The pair slid around the old tower until they reached the splintered door. Maurice watched as Julien sniffed the air once more, seeming to read vibrations on the subtle plane, and pointed to the lock. Maurice shook his head sharply in protest, for there were too many guards within earshot.

But Julien smiled and twitched his fingers in the air. Maurice let out an agitated sigh and nodded, darting his eyes around in careful watch. Then, in order both to act and to experiment, to discover what powers he possessed by way of exercising them, Julien bent his fingers and made a clawing motion towards the lock. A tiny bit of violet light, just enough for the task, shot from his fingertips to interact with the lock, which unlatched and fell to the ground with a clang precisely at the moment an owl hooted loudly.

The men quietly pushed the door ajar and slipped inside. Julien waited in the pitch blackness while Maurice fumbled in the sack for candles and matches, whispering that it smelled of something more than just evil. He illuminated the darkness as together, in musical harmony, the pair pronounced, "Absinthe."

Lifting the light above their heads, they found themselves at the top of a set of stone stairs that wound downward against the wall through a fog of cobwebs to the dungeon. When they reached the bottom their olfactory instincts were confirmed. Broken glass crunched beneath their feet as they meandered through stacks of boxes all bearing the logo "*Demos: The People's Absinthe.*"

They crunched across the floor into the next room, where enormous rusted vats stood amid jars filled with rotted plants labeled with graphology suggesting dementia.

"The poison breed of wormwood," Maurice observed. "But it looks unused since the turn of the century. It had done its job: the people were poisoned, the king was dead, and Regina was sieging the throne."

Just then Julien felt a chill not of sorcery, but of something cold beckoning his astral body. He followed the vibration down a hallway of barred cells leading to an open doorway. The men held their candles high and entered the dungeon's final chamber, where on the far wall was a downward-facing pentagram to which a skeleton was tied, its head pointed to the floor.

The rest of the room was empty save for a fire-pit at the base of the star with incense, bones, and a book of diabolic incantations. Maurice knelt down to inspect the altar, holding up his candle to decipher the text before gasping in horror.

Julien knelt beside him and read the deranged scrawling written in charcoal on a wooden board:

Here rests the patriarch Le Comte de la Tour-Abolie

Sacrificed to our Lord and Master

The Prince-

iple

of

Darkness

April 30, 1896

Julien said he had seen all he needed to see and the pair made their way back through the dungeon. But just before they reached the staircase they were stopped by the sound of crunching glass and the cry, "Who goes there?"

At the base of the steps stood one of the hideous ones: corpulent, asymmetric, with metal-gouged nose and indeterminate gender. Julien waved his claws, sending crackles of violet-colored violence across the chamber, which struck the fiendish foe, surrounding it with electro-magnetic light and sending it convulsing to the floor.

The men stood over it, and by the light of their candles beheld lacerations on every inch of the thing, like a map of its circulatory system. Blood oozed until the mapping was no longer discernible and all they could see was a crimson corpse. Maurice warned that there could be more coming any second and hastily prepared the Sword of Achilles invocation, summoning the great warrior and his faithful followers to immediately cross the threshold from the overworld.

In their mutual state of *mag*, he and Julien willed that when they climbed the stairs and exited the tower Achilles and the myrmidons would greet them. The rites complete, Julien scaled the steps with Maurice close behind, burst through the open doorway, and drew his sword.

Throughout the gardens, nine myrmidons were drawing their swords as well—from the bodies of their victims—while Achilles stood on the edge of the fountain, decapitating the telluric totem. Julien rushed to him and the two embraced with a grappling hold. Then Julien waved his sword and the band of brothers trotted across the gardens, the myrmidons scanning every corner for guards, every window for watchful eyes.

When they reached the castle door Maurice and Julien debated magical options for entry, but Achilles scoffed and motioned to a myrmidon, who dissolved into the ether, slipped through the illusion of the door's material reality, coagulated on the other side, and pushed it open. The dozen men stepped inside the great hall, where witches appeared within moments, summoning fairy-demons from the miasma of their sorcery.

Julien neutralized the green demons with violet light, while Achilles and the myrmidons executed the witches. With sounds of alarm from above, Julien and Maurice bounded up the staircase just as a pair of double-doors slammed shut on the room from which Julien had emerged that fateful Walpurgis Night. Julien shocked the lock and kicked the doors open.

Regina stood across the room behind a desk stacked with matriarchal proclamations, and sent green goop through the Universal Plastic Medium. Julien stood impassively as the slime-light reached the area around his heart, then bounced off with a wave of repulsion. Regina cast her spell again, followed by a third time, but the viscous light would not penetrate Julien, and came to rest, as if concussed, floating in the air.

"Impossible!" Regina shouted.

Julien curled the fingers on his left hand, which glowed royal purple, and with a sudden thrust sent Regina's sickening sorcery back at her, knocking her into her chair subdued and panting as the slime crawled about her and did its work.

She stared at Julien with a sneer of absolute defiance and complete negation, as Julien inspected the toll two decades of witchcraft had taken. Regina's aged face had been altered with every kind of sinister artificiality in order to appear youthful to the hapless masses, but she could not prevent her body from descending into matter, and her belly and thighs were corpulent. The sound of running steps and swords slicing bone echoed across the upper floor of the château, then the screams abruptly ended and the myrmidons came bursting into the room.

"Who are these clowns?" crowed Regina.

"I take it you're going to burn the witch?" said Achilles calmly.

Maurice wanted it done then and there, but Julien had another notion of divine justice, saying they should end her reign in the ballroom, the place where she had killed the king and usurped his throne. He told Maurice to search the rooms for something suitable for her to wear — something for the devil's whore.

Maurice departed as the myrmidons dragged Regina kicking and screaming down the stairs. Julien led the way to the ballroom, where he found the low stage upon which he had sung at his grand masquerade, now occupied by a podium where Regina announced her proclamations to the press.

"You cannot stop us!" she screamed. "Everything shall be the same — ugly — everyone shall be free — in bondage — and all shall be equal — under Satan!"

Maurice came into the ballroom with an armful of clothes and cosmetics, asking if they would suffice. Julien nodded his approval, and, with swords at her throat, the myrmidons forced Regina to don a red bustier, stockings, and a pair of fluffy boudoir slippers, while Julien smeared her lips with rouge.

Regina's cold regard betrayed her deepest thoughts, that she was being demoted from empress to harlot by a hero and band of warriors, conquered by the divine order for which she secretly longed.

"Julien, *tempus fugit!*" shouted Maurice.

The myrmidons looked deferentially to Achilles, who grabbed Regina by the arm, spanked her flabby buttocks, and pulled her up to the podium. She began speaking in tongues, blabbering all the guttural gobbledygook of demonic possession. Achilles forced her to kneel, grabbed her by the hair, and pulled her head back.

Julien stepped onto the stage, adjusted his cloak, and raised his sword above his head. Slowly he inverted it, holding the handle in his violet-glowing hands, the point angled down, before driving it into Regina's gullet and entrails. Blood spewed from her mouth as Julien twisted the blade, grinding it against her ribcage and cracking off teeth. Then he withdrew his sword and decapitated the demon-empress, sending her head flying off the stage and rolling across the floor.

Achilles suggested they cast it into the sea. Maurice retrieved the bloody head and threw it into Julien's knapsack, and the twelve men exited the château as the sound of motorcars and sirens echoed in the distance. When Julien said he must go to the Alps, he and Maurice LeBlanc knew it would be the last time they ever saw each other.

"Can you make it through the forest?" said Julien.

Maurice nodded.

"Then go, my friend, and may the Regal Light shine ever upon you."

Julien next turned to the great warrior. "I feel like I should be able to fly," he said with frustration. "When do I gain the power?"

"When you say, 'I should be able to fly,' is when you are ready to fly," replied Achilles. "We can show you, but it will mark a point of no return, the beginning of the end of your earthly life and the start of your ascension."

The sound of sirens grew louder, and lights flashed through the rickety fence surrounding the garden.

"Do it," said Julien, knowing he had done all he could in the Age of Iron.

Achilles put his hand on his shoulder and all grew dark save for a glowing circuitry of electro-magnetic light—the same that had projected from Julien's hands. There was a sense of effortless velocity, and then, in what seemed like just a few seconds, he found himself standing at the end of a stone bridge with a majestic castle before him. Snow was falling, and the township below was engulfed in flames.

"Go to your kindred while you can," said Achilles. "The state of Being through which you have just passed is beyond life and death, and you will soon shed your mortal coil."

As snowflakes gathered in the curls of his beard, Julien asked whether he was now immortal. Achilles told him he would need one more thing in order to ascend to the Olympian dimension: an Apple of the Hesperides. Julien felt a chill of horrified failure, having forgotten to retrieve it in Hellas, but Achilles smiled and placed one in Julien's hand, compliments of Ares.

Peering up in wonder at the great alpine castle, Achilles pronounced the edifice magnificent. The men clasped each other's forearms and exchanged bittersweet smiles as the smell of smoke from below filled their nostrils.

"The beard suits you, by the way," said Achilles.

"To the bond between gods and men," replied Julien.

"To the bond between gods and men."

The great warrior and his nine followers dissolved into the ether, leaving only their footprints in the snow. Julien raced across the bridge in the howling wind, passing through the doors of the Gothic masterpiece that had been ripped down from the stars centuries before to fill the hearts of its builders. Inside all was silent. Scattered torches and candles shone like the starlights of the masquerading spirit-helpers who had guided Julien through his earthly incarnation, protecting him until such time that he would reach his spiritual homeland high in the snow-capped mountains.

"I'm here!" a voice echoed through the castle.

Julien searched for its source down a long corridor flanked with suits of armor and statues of Hellenic maidens, which formed a zigzag pattern of alternating masculine and feminine figures of light and dark. A light shone at the end of the corridor, and when Julien crossed the threshold he found himself inside a library lined with empty shelves stretched to the ceiling.

"Do you remember when we first met?" said Zoe from behind a walnut table across the room, illumined by a single silver candelabrum.

"As though it were yesterday, my child," replied Julien. "Even if it was 22 years ago."

"The magic number once more," smiled Zoe. "And how old I was at the time, just a naive girl with drawings for a book of Tarot. This was my illustration for The Emperor, the final card in the spread we drew on our voyage of destiny."

Julien crossed the room as Zoe slid the card across the table. He raised it, beholding a figure whose likeness he had now become: a bearded sovereign of equal parts will and power, sensibility and fecundity, with a cloak like the one he wore now, and holding a sword like the one that hung from his hip. A Gothic window framed the figure, while the rectangular border of the card was executed in a Grecian key motif. Julien set the card down with a smile, gazing fondly at his fellow traveler, the soul-sister he had met at the beginning and to whom he had returned in the end.

Zoe Wingate had mastered alchemy on her own path to become a true priestess and guardian of the Primordial Tradition. The Supreme Author had shown her a way reserved only for the rarest of the rare, an honor granted to earthly women who pledged themselves not to the elemental forces of Mother Earth, but the eternal wisdom of the Sky Father, from whom Mother Earth derives. Zoe was serene, possessed of both great wisdom and great assertion thanks to her powers of virgin creation. Having passed from pixie to fairy queen, she bore gray-streaked hair that fell to her waist.

Julien set the apple on the table, removed his cloak and sword-belt, and the two shared an embrace filled with love and kinship from higher dimensions.

"The township is on fire, my dear," he said with a fatal smile.

"And soon they will be coming for us," said Zoe, resigned but resilient. "They know that for centuries this castle has guarded something they do not understand and do not value, which is precisely why they do not understand it."

Julien asked who "they" was.

"Everyone not like us, my darling. Down the mountain rampages a multi-headed hydra of capitalists and peasants, bolsheviks and degenerates, witches and warlocks, Christians, Muslims, and Jews. They are all enemies of the regal spirit that lives within you and I."

"Achilles said he would not fight for the men of today," said Julien, "but he would fight for me — and he did."

"The deed is done?"

"The deed is done."

"And you flew here?"

"I did."

"Then you are truly a hero," said Zoe, kissing his cheek. "If only it would halt the decadence. But now that we've reached the end, all my powers have concentrated into a single revelation. What I was seeing just now in the Astral Light was more demonic than anything I've seen before. I perceived a rectangular object which I understood was called a 'screen.' On this screen played out all the cancerous corruption plaguing the soul of our people. All of Europa shall be ruled by tyrants orchestrating a barbarian invasion. Paris, Londontown, Berlin, Brussels, Amsterdam, Rome, Milan, Stockholm, Madrid, Lisbon—all of them will smolder while robots fly through the smoke-filled skies, the armies of Allah go about their lives unfazed, and the children of Moses count their gold.

"A century from now," Zoe continued, "all we took for granted—all that a refined soul of taste and intelligence could actualize—will be as fictitious as a fairy tale, something the people of the future will think could never possibly have existed."

"It all starts in the land and sky," waxed Julien solemnly. "It's the seasons, the forest and deer, the sea and the birds. It's high noon in Hellas and midnight in Germania. From this sensibility of sun and moon sprout castles and masquerades, opera and ballet, the taverns where poets drink wine and gardens where tales are told to children, tilling the soil of their imaginations with fantasy and wonder. It's old houses where the ghosts of the past creak with the furniture, the art of the sword and the elegance of the waltz. It's family and honor and everything noble and good, free from the cult of the savior, the lie of equality, and the poison of commerce. I love it all, my sweet, and as a sheath must be equal to its sword, so do I despise everything that stands against it."

"This is why you were destined to be king," said Zoe. "Because your heart is great enough to love it all. And that is why from the moment I saw you I knew I could love only you, my lord and king, and that no other earthly man should ever know me."

As the sands in the hourglass of his life trickled down, Julien grew ever more wistful. "Why can we not have grand balls in elegant palaces and still honor the gods?" he said. "Can there not be mansions of opulence and luxury at the end of gravel roadways lined with statues of the Muses? Can there not be horseless carriages that are sleek and powerful, but named Apollo and not Diablo? Can not everything emanating from our creative wellspring be concentrated like cinnabar, with the sword ever vigilant against the armies of darkness? The dark, demonic, telluric tribes of mankind, who wreak upon us all that is corrosive, destroying, subverting, inverting, negating, uglifying and ignorance-making? And cannot this great re-conquest of the Primordial Tradition take place in the heart of every man of Spirit, above the serfs and merchants, as it has in mine?"

"That is the world you must make, Julien Stanwyck," said Zoe, stroking his arm. "All that you've gathered and learned, selected and refined. The soul of our people, crystallized into cinnabar, re-ignited in the heavens. Mount Olympus raised Gothically, from the depths of the Decadence, reborn with dark love and dark power. Build that world and the souls will come, and the gods will awaken."

Pivoting on the volatility that was part of his soul in eternity, Julien tore the sword on the table from its scabbard, swung it through the air with menace, and demanded to know why Zapfe had sent him on a fool's errand. "If I cannot save the world," he snarled with a wrath that shook the castle's stones, "what was the point of it all?"

"Why, immortality for you and me, my lord and love!" cried Zoe with tears in her eyes. "We who saw what others could not, we who venerated what others cast away. And even though escape-by-ascension is our only option, we can rebuild in the Astral Light—and rain hellfire down upon our enemies. From the place where we'll soon be, it won't matter whether it's a hundred years from now or ten thousand. And a deity awaits you on the other side, Julien, and she's your bride."

"What will we be on the other side?" Julien asked, gently waving the sword in the candlelight.

"Angels, muses, spirits — no one in this realm has ever known for sure. We will ascend the Great Chain of Being back towards the Supreme Author, and discover his next role for us."

Zoe took the apple in her hand, courageously and without emotion, and Julien asked whether they would ascend together.

"From what I've come to understand in my heart as Truth," said Zoe, "my spirit will follow an individuated process of ascension. I will find you when you and your sister have created a current within the Astral Light, a new Gothic kingdom in the Olympian dimension, born of the royal blood of divine siblings."

Zoe watched as Julien's bronzed face turned pale, and sighed deeply, for she knew instantly why.

"I thought *you* were my soul-sister, my kindred of the spirit," said Julien. "Achilles just called you such."

"We are *all* kindred spirits," said Zoe, "but Darlena is the sister-bride destined for you if you succeeded in your mission. Years ago Zapfe explained that you were the last initiate into the Royal Art, the one who would be wedded through the *conjunction mysteriis* and given an occult bride on the subtle plane in order to become king in another realm. Julien, as sure as Zeus sired you with lightning that night in Gaul through your mother and the Comte de la Tour-Abolie, so did he order the generation of Darlena. Was there not a crack of lightning in the Valley of the Queens? Zeus came to Aphrodite Scorpia, loved her, and made a bride of divine lineage for his hero. And now, my lord, that extra Tarot card I asked you to take all those years ago. The one I said would help interpret the others when the time was right — will you tell me what it was?"

"The Wheel of Fortune."

"Then you know what we must do."

Julien nodded, raised his sword, and dealt a regal blow to the apple on the table, splitting it in two. "To immortality," he said, taking his half.

"To immortality," echoed Zoe, taking hers.

"The world is for merchants and slaves," said Julien with a hearty bite. "Olympus is for kings."

OTHER BOOKS PUBLISHED BY ARKTOS

Virginia Abernethy	*Born Abroad*
Sri Dharma Pravartaka Acharya	*The Dharma Manifesto*
Joakim Andersen	*Rising from the Ruins*
Winston C. Banks	*Excessive Immigration*
Stephen Baskerville	*Who Lost America?*
Alfred Baeumler	*Nietzsche: Philosopher and Politician*
Matt Battaglioli	*The Consequences of Equality*
Alain de Benoist	*Beyond Human Rights* *Carl Schmitt Today* *The Ideology of Sameness* *The Indo-Europeans* *Manifesto for a European Renaissance* *On the Brink of the Abyss* *The Problem of Democracy* *Runes and the Origins of Writing* *View from the Right* (vol. 1–3)
Armand Berger	*Tolkien, Europe, and Tradition*
Pawel Bielawski	*European Apostasy*
Arthur Moeller van den Bruck	*Germany's Third Empire*
Kerry Bolton	*The Perversion of Normality* *Revolution from Above* *Yockey: A Fascist Odyssey*
Isac Boman	*Money Power*
Daniel Branco	*The Absolute Philosopher*
Charles William Dailey	*The Serpent Symbol in Tradition*
Antoine Dresse	*Political Realism*
Ricardo Duchesne	*Faustian Man in a Multicultural Age*
Alexander Dugin	*Ethnos and Society* *Ethnosociology* *Eurasian Mission* *The Fourth Political Theory* *The Great Awakening vs the Great Reset* *Last War of the World-Island* *Politica Aeterna* *Political Platonism* *Putin vs Putin* *The Rise of the Fourth Political Theory* *The Trump Revolution* *Templars of the Proletariat* *The Theory of a Multipolar World*
Daria Dugina	*A Theory of Europe*
Edward Dutton	*Race Differences in Ethnocentrism*
Mark Dyal	*Hated and Proud*
Clare Ellis	*The Blackening of Europe* (vol. 1–3)
Koenraad Elst	*Return of the Swastika*
Julius Evola	*The Bow and the Club* *Fascism Viewed from the Right* *A Handbook for Right-Wing Youth* *Metaphysics of Power* *Metaphysics of War* *The Myth of the Blood*

OTHER BOOKS PUBLISHED BY ARKTOS

	Notes on the Third Reich
	Pagan Imperialism
	Recognitions
	A Traditionalist Confronts Fascism
Guillaume Faye	*Against Russophobia*
	Archeofuturism
	Archeofuturism 2.0
	The Colonisation of Europe
	Convergence of Catastrophes
	Ethnic Apocalypse
	A Global Coup
	Prelude to War
	Sex and Deviance
	Understanding Islam
	Why We Fight
Daniel S. Forrest	*Suprahumanism*
Andrew Fraser	*Dissident Dispatches*
	Reinventing Aristocracy in the Age of Woke Capital
	The WASP Question
Génération Identitaire	*We are Generation Identity*
Peter Goodchild	*The Taxi Driver from Baghdad*
	The Western Path
Paul Gottfried	*War and Democracy*
Georges Guiscard	*White Privilege*
Petr Hampl	*Breached Enclosure*
Porus Homi Havewala	*The Saga of the Aryan Race*
Richard Houck	*Liberalism Unmasked*
A. J. Illingworth	*Political Justice*
Institut Iliade	*For a European Awakening*
	Guardians of Heritage
Alexander Jacob	*De Naturae Natura*
Jason Reza Jorjani	*Artemis Unveiled*
	Closer Encounters
	Erosophia
	Faustian Futurist
	Iranian Leviathan
	Lovers of Sophia
	Metapolemos
	Novel Folklore
	Philosophy of the Future
	Prometheism
	Promethean Pirate
	Prometheus and Atlas
	Psychotron
	Thanosis
	Uber Man
	World State of Emergency
Henrik Jonasson	*Sigmund*
Edgar Julius Jung	*The Significance of the German Revolution*
Ruuben Kaalep & August Meister	*Rebirth of Europe*
Lance Kennedy	*The Book of the Scribe*
James Kirkpatrick	*Conservatism Inc.*

OTHER BOOKS PUBLISHED BY ARKTOS

Ludwig Klages	*The Biocentric Worldview*
	Cosmogonic Reflections
	The Science of Character
Andrew Korybko	*Hybrid Wars*
Pierre Krebs	*Guillaume Faye: Truths & Tributes*
	Fighting for the Essence
Julien Langella	*Catholic and Identitarian*
Henri Levavasseur	*Identity: The Foundation of the City*
John Bruce Leonard	*The New Prometheans*
Diana Panchenko	*The Inevitable*
Jean-Yves Le Gallou	*The Propaganda Society*
Stephen Pax Leonard	*The Ideology of Failure*
	Travels in Cultural Nihilism
William S. Lind	*Reforging Excalibur*
	Retroculture
Pentti Linkola	*Can Life Prevail?*
Giorgio Locchi	*Definitions*
H. P. Lovecraft	*The Conservative*
Norman Lowell	*Imperium Europa*
Richard Lynn	*Sex Differences in Intelligence*
	A Tribute to Helmut Nyborg (ed.)
John MacLugash	*The Return of the Solar King*
Charles Maurras	*The Future of the Intelligentsia & For a French Awakening*
Graeme Maxton	*The Follies of the Western Mind*
John Harmon McElroy	*Agitprop in America*
Michael O'Meara	*Guillaume Faye and the Battle of Europe*
	New Culture, New Right
Michael Millerman	*Beginning with Heidegger*
Dmitry Moiseev	*The Philosophy of Italian Fascism*
Maurice Muret	*The Greatness of Elites*
Brian Anse Patrick	*The NRA and the Media*
	Rise of the Anti-Media
	The Ten Commandments of Propaganda
	Zombology
Tito Perdue	*The Bent Pyramid*
	Journey to a Location
	Lee
	Morning Crafts
	Philip
	The Sweet-Scented Manuscript
	William's House (vol. 1–4)
John K. Press	*The True West vs the Zombie Apocalypse*
Raido	*A Handbook of Traditional Living* (vol. 1–2)
P R Reddall	*Towards Awakening*
Claire Rae Randall	*The War on Gender*
Steven J. Rosen	*The Agni and the Ecstasy*
	The Jedi in the Lotus
Nicholas Rooney	*Talking to the Wolf*

OTHER BOOKS PUBLISHED BY ARKTOS

Richard Rudgley	*Barbarians* *Essential Substances* *Wildest Dreams*
Ernst von Salomon	*It Cannot Be Stormed* *The Outlaws*
Werner Sombart	*Traders and Heroes*
Piero San Giorgio	*Giuseppe* *Survive the Economic Collapse* *Surviving the Next Catastrophe*
Sri Sri Ravi Shankar	*Celebrating Silence* *Know Your Child* *Management Mantras* *Patanjali Yoga Sutras* *Secrets of Relationships*
Oswald Spengler	*The Decline of the West* *Man and Technics*
Richard Storey	*The Uniqueness of Western Law*
J. R. Sommer	*The New Colossus*
Tomislav Sunic	*Against Democracy and Equality* *Homo Americanus* *Postmortem Report* *Titans are in Town*
Askr Svarte	*Gods in the Abyss*
Hans-Jürgen Syberberg	*On the Fortunes and Misfortunes of Art in Post-War Germany*
Abir Taha	*Defining Terrorism* *The Epic of Arya* (2nd ed.) *Nietzsche is Coming God, or the Redemption of the Divine* *Verses of Light*
Jean Thiriart	*Europe: An Empire of 400 Million*
Bal Gangadhar Tilak	*The Arctic Home in the Vedas*
Bostian Marco Turk	*War in the Name of Peace*
Dominique Venner	*Ernst Jünger: A Different European Destiny* *For a Positive Critique* *The Shock of History*
Hans Vogel	*How Europe Became American*
Tim Vorgens	*Legitimate Preference*
Markus Willinger	*A Europe of Nations* *Generation Identity*
Alexander Wolfheze	*Alba Rosa* *Globus Horribilis* *Rupes Nigra*

www.ingramcontent.com/pod-product-compliance
Lightning Source LLC
LaVergne TN
LVHW051000080826
845145LV00009B/2381

* 9 7 8 1 9 1 8 4 1 8 1 4 9 *